EL DIABLO

EVERNIGHT PUBLISHING ®

www.evernightpublishing.com

Copyright© 2019

Sam Crescent and Stacey Espino

Editor: Karyn White

Cover Art: Jay Aheer

ISBN: 978-1-77339-945-4

EL DIABLO

EL DIABLO

Killer of Kings, 6

Sam Crescent and Stacey Espino

Copyright © 2018

〜・・◆・〜

Chapter One

Xavier slid the patio door closed behind him, careful not to make a sound. The rich scent of coffee wafted in the air. Most people loved the smell. He fucking hated it. He pushed away childhood memories of picking coffee beans in his bare feet for twelve grueling hours a day. Right now, he needed to stay focused.

He was there to kill a man.

The oceanfront paradise belonged to a dirty trader. He'd pissed off the wrong people, spreading rumors and creating false market values. The men who'd lost millions because of him had hired Killer of Kings for some swift justice.

Xavier had been working for the notorious group of hitmen for over ten months now. He'd done his training with Chains and Killian, and he'd been fulfilling contracts for a few months. The work paid well, so he couldn't complain.

Lazy footsteps shuffled down the hallway. He twisted a silencer onto the end of his Glock, not liking the leather gloves Boss insisted he wear. Mr. Strogonov wasn't expecting him this morning. Nobody wanted a visit from El Diablo.

He watched as the man lifted the carafe from the coffeemaker and poured himself a drink. He wore a plush navy bathrobe and matching slippers, humming a carefree tune as he puttered around the kitchen. Strogonov was forty-three, only a few years older than Xavier himself. The bastard had some city miles, probably from the stress of ripping off his associates. When he turned around and noticed Xavier sitting at his dining table, he dropped the mug, the ceramic pieces scattering on the marble floor.

"Who are you?" His voice trembled, his lower lip quivering.

"Who do you think I am?"

The man looked from side to side, then reached for his neck.

"Your personal alert won't work. I've already deactivated it. You didn't think they'd hire an amateur, did you?"

"W-who hired you?"

Xavier smirked. "You have more than one enemy? You've been busy." He waved an arm in the air. "Stealing certainly pays well, doesn't it?"

"I never stole anything."

He set his gun on the glass tabletop with care, then stood up, slowly pushing the chair back into place. He rolled out his shoulders. "You're far from innocent, Mr. Strogonov."

"I can pay you. Whatever they're giving you, I'll do better. Name your price."

There was no reason for him to talk to this guy. Strogonov could beg and cry and offer him the world. It wouldn't do any good once Killer of Kings was contracted. This was more than money; it was about reputation, respect, and getting the job done. He'd spent a lot of time with Boss and his men over the past year, and for the first time in his life, he felt connected. Being on top, ruling with an iron fist in some of the most ruthless gangs and cartels never fulfilled him. It only added to the loneliness, the disconnect he'd always felt. Chains and the other players at Killer of Kings were his equals, and the level playing field was surprisingly satisfying.

"I need you to write a confession letter. Go on, grab a paper and pen. I'll wait."

"What for?"

He took a deep breath and exhaled. "Don't make me ask you twice."

The man scrambled around the kitchen, opening and closing drawers. Sweat beaded on his forehead, highlighting his receding hairline.

"The top drawer beside the sink," he said. "And bring a glass of water back with you." Xavier had already scoped out this place, and taken all the steps to ensure the contract went smooth and clean. He had something to prove to Boss. Once the man had the pad, pen, and water, he continued, "Now, you're going to apologize and spell out exactly what you did to alter the market."

Once he had the suicide note, he could finish this hit. His gun was only a precaution.

"I can't do that. They'll lock me away for the rest of my life."

He shook his head. Jail was the last thing this bastard should be worried about. "Do you know what they called me back in Colombia?" Xavier massaged one of the man's shoulders, making him flinch. "El Diablo. If you don't know, that means The Devil. Some said I was a sociopath, that I lacked empathy. Others were more blunt, calling me a monster. Maybe they were right. But monsters aren't born—they're made." He could have gone on, talking about his bullshit childhood, being sold to the *barrio* gang to pay a debt his mother owed. About the little sister torn from his arms. Sometimes he unloaded it all, knowing whoever he told was about to meet their maker. It was his therapy, a confession of his sins. He shoved Strogonov down into a chair. The man whimpered. "You don't want to piss me off." The trip down memory lane plus a wicked case of blue balls had put him in a less than stellar mood.

Once everything had been written out, Xavier neatly folded the paper and tucked it into the breast pocket of Mr. Strogonov's robe. "Very good," he said. "Now take these with the water." He set two pills on the table beside the glass.

"What are they?"

"Don't worry about it. Take the damn pills." He picked up his gun to punctuate this sentence.

Within minutes of swallowing the lethal drugs, Strogonov slumped over the glass table, the water spilling.

Drip, drip, drip off the edge onto the marble floors.

This job was too easy. Xavier liked to use his gun or knives, something challenging where he could let off steam. But Boss wanted a textbook suicide, so he delivered.

He walked to the kitchen window. The view above the sink was breathtaking, clouds tinted with pink and orange reflected on the ocean's surface. It was way too fucking early to be awake.

Xavier tucked his Glock into his shoulder harness and left the way he came. Strogonov had an ex-wife and no children. Even if he'd had a family, it wouldn't have changed the outcome. Xavier was fucked up in the head, always had been. He never felt guilt or regret when killing. Maybe he was numb to the bloodshed … or he really was a monster.

Once he got to his car, settling back against the soft leather, he called Boss.

"Job's done."

"You're on a roll," said Boss. "I have another contract for tomorrow. You'll love this one."

He scrubbed his hand over the stubble on his jaw. "Oh?"

"You'll have to get your hands dirty. I'll email you the details." The line went dead.

Boss never was one for small talk. If you did your job well, you got more work, and he left you alone. If you fucked up, he'd ride your ass. He demanded perfection and rarely gave second chances. The man had a reputation for a reason.

The only reason Xavier started this job was in exchange for information about his sister. Boss had given him a few leads, but nothing that panned out. He kept promising more, but after a year of waiting, Xavier was starting to wonder.

The highway drive was usually a bumper to bumper nightmare, but this early in the morning, it was relatively clear. He hit the gas and headed home. Over the past few months, he'd made more money than most men earned in a lifetime. Hitmen with good track records made a very lucrative living. But chasing the almighty dollar was a road leading to nowhere. He knew that well, but it didn't stop him either. He had nothing to lose.

Forty minutes later, he drove along his winding

driveway. His home was a modern marvel, set on a vast acreage. He valued his privacy and security. By now he knew money couldn't buy happiness, but he always had something to prove. As if owning the best was the measure of a man, or could erase the memories of living in the slums of District 4 of Soacha.

The only thing that marred the perfect landscape was the little yellow Kia with rust around the fenders. It belonged to the live-in housekeeper he'd hired a few months ago. Once his training was over, he had no time for anything on the home front. She had her own living area on the far east wing of the mansion. Ms. Alesha Sanders knew not to enter his office, the basement, or to leave her live-in suite after hours. Keeping a civilian on his payroll wasn't recommended, but sometimes it was nice to play normal and get away from all the bullshit.

He'd interviewed over a dozen potential housekeepers. Xavier had no time for anything but his contracts. He needed a woman to cook, clean, and keep his domestic affairs in order. The interviews were on a downward spiral until Alesha sat across from his desk.

She was young and curvy with freckles across her nose. Her lips were full and pouty, and he doubted she knew how tempting she was. She wore a plain cotton dress with a white cardigan. He wasn't sure what it was about her, but he knew she was the one for the job.

Of course, he had Maurice do a full work up on her. She'd been living on her own since she was eighteen. No criminal record. No dependents. Ms. Alesha was a twenty-seven-year-old waitress turned housekeeper. Her references were impeccable, but he'd already decided to hire her before doing the background check.

Some days he regretted his decision to hire her because he hadn't been able to bring women home knowing she was under the same roof. He wasn't sure why she kept messing with his head. Alesha was a housekeeper, not his fucking wife.

So far, she'd kept her distance and followed the rules. It would be a shame if he had to kill her.

****

Keeping her boss happy was Alesha's number one priority. Getting this job had been no less than winning the lottery. She had her own suite, something so beautiful she almost cried when he gave her the tour. The pay was incredible. Her boss was hardly home, and never bothered her. Alesha had her fair share of nightmarish encounters with men when she'd waitressed at a few local bars. It didn't take long for her to change careers. She couldn't stand strange men touching her or constantly propositioning her. Her coworkers may have enjoyed the attention, but it only made her sick. There weren't too many options without a secondary education, and fancy diplomas weren't made for people barely able to pay the rent, never mind tuition and books.

She'd been doing well as a cleaner for the last eight years, but it wasn't until being hired by Xavier Moreno that things really started looking up. Her situation seemed too perfect, to the point that she constantly worried he'd lay her off or fire her for screwing something up.

He'd gone out much earlier than normal today, so she decided to prepare a special dinner, something that required more prep time than usual. His tastes could be demanding, and she tried hard to make things he'd enjoy as she learned his likes and dislikes. By now, she knew he detested coffee and didn't like onions in his eggs. Every day was a learning experience.

As she peeled some carrots by the sink, the security alarm dinged, signaling someone had entered through the front door.

He was home.

Her heart began to race. Yes, he was her boss, but she'd be lying if she said she only had platonic feelings for him. The man was an enigma, rarely talking to her, coming and going at the strangest hours. She still had no clue what he did for a living, and didn't dare ask and risk pissing him off. He was very private, and made it crystal clear when he'd hired her.

She did find it odd that a man his age with both looks and money was living alone in such a big house. There were no family photos, no visits from relatives, and he'd never brought a woman home that she knew of. Even though he gave her every other weekend off with full pay, she rarely left her suite. Where would she even go? This was as close to home as she had. Even her own mother had wiped the slate clean nine years ago when she married her new husband, and that included Alesha. They hadn't spoken since.

Of course, it secretly pleased her that Xavier never brought home dates. It kept her fantasy alive, the one where he fell madly in love with his maid. She giggled under her breath.

"Something funny?"

She dropped her peeler into the sink with a clang and whirled around, wiping her hands on her apron. "Nothing, sir. I didn't hear you come in."

"Don't call me sir. It makes me feel old." He tossed his keys on the counter with a jangle and shrugged off his jacket. Her eyes darted to the gun strapped to his body, and she froze in place. He noticed her staring and looked down. "Relax, it's registered. A man can't be too safe these days." He winked at her.

Of course. A man like Xavier Moreno would be a target for criminals. She'd just never seen a gun in real life. "I'm sorry, sir."

He frowned and crossed his arms. "Alesha…"

"I'm sorry … Mr. Moreno."

"You can call me Xavier. I won't bite."

Xavier. Just hearing him say his own name with his slight accent made her wet. He was pure masculinity, confident, and drool-worthy. This was probably the most time she'd spent with him since being hired. He was usually gone before she started working in the kitchen, she wasn't allowed in the main house after nine at night, and he always came home late.

He dropped down in one of the dining chairs and loosened his collar. He had intricate tattoos that climbed up his neck, and she had to stop herself from staring. "You were up early this morning," she said, trying to start some small talk.

"I had a business meeting with a new client. Way too early for my liking. I think I'll go back to bed for a couple hours."

"You did go to sleep late last night." She bit the inside of her cheek, wishing she could take back her words. Xavier loved his privacy, and she sounded like a stalker.

"You're observant."

He stood up, cracking his neck to each side.

"Sorry, the walls are thin and I'm a light sleeper."

"I'll keep that in mind," he said. Xavier started walking away.

Alesha wanted to tell him to stay, to talk to her, to tell her more about himself. She loved the subtle scent of his cologne since he'd entered the kitchen. Her entire body took notice of everything Xavier, from his commanding presence to the intensity in his dark eyes. But she kept quiet and picked up her peeler. *You're such a chicken shit, Alesha.*

Just before he left the kitchen, she summoned up enough courage. "Could you do me a favor before you leave?"

"What is it?"

She held out a glass jar. "Can you open this?"

He eyed her skeptically.

As he approached, she realized just how tall and buff he was, his shoulders and biceps straining against the fabric of his shirt. She couldn't help but stare at the gun now that it was within arm's length. It unnerved her. Xavier took the jar and twisted it open with ease, then set it on the counter. He didn't move away.

When she looked up to gauge his expression, he pulled the gun from its holster. She gasped. "This scares you?" he asked. He released the clip and checked the chamber, then handed it to her. "Take it."

Alesha shook her head. "No, I can't."

"It's unloaded. You won't conquer your fears unless you face them." He reached down and grabbed her wrist, pressing the gun into her palm. It was cold and heavy against her skin. She wrapped her fingers around the handle, still afraid even though it was rendered harmless. She wondered if Xavier was afraid of anything. "Good girl. There you go."

He moved behind her until her back was pressed to his body. Xavier reached around her sides, enveloping her, bringing her arms straight out in front of her. Every move was slow and deliberate. Her body thrummed, her cheeks heating. He bent over enough so that his face was next to hers. She even felt a brief brush of his stubble on her skin.

"Just like that," he whispered close to her ear. "Look through the sights and aim at your target. Never hesitate. Take a breath and pull." He placed his finger over hers and pulled the trigger. The gun made a sharp click, and she jumped. "It's okay, I've got you."

She wanted to melt into his arms. The heat of his body warmed her bare skin, but she still broke out into gooseflesh. "I think it's safer in your hands," she said, returning the pistol to him.

He grabbed the clip and then returned the gun to his holster as if he'd done it a thousand times. "You're a natural, Alesha. I'll have to give you lessons."

Her name sounded perfect on his lips. "That sounds like fun." No, it didn't. Guns terrified her, but she wanted another chance to be close to Xavier. A one on one lesson sounded intimate, even though she was certain he was just being a nice guy.

"You're jumpy. I just want you to know you never have to worry while living here. No one will ever hurt you."

It was an odd thing to say, but she liked the confidence in his voice. He made her feel safe. Alesha hoped she hadn't crossed any boundaries. Maybe the lesson was a bad idea. The last thing she needed was for things to get awkward between them and for her to lose her job as a result.

"I'm very happy working here," she said for good measure.

"The place has never been cleaner."

Disappointment assaulted her. She was just the damn maid, and she had to remember that. He was any woman's wet dream. Alesha tucked her fantasies back into her imagination where they belonged.

Chapter Two

The last thing Xavier should be doing was showing his very sexy housekeeper how to hold a gun. That was a big mistake on his part. What he also didn't like was the look of disappointment in her eyes when he said the house had never been cleaner. What did he miss?

How could a compliment make her react that way?

He was trying to be nice, not something he usually bothered with.

Until she came along, his home had been a shithole.

Honestly, he didn't like picking up after himself, and because he had plenty of money, when he was done with clothes, he tossed them. There was no time in his life for dirty laundry, cleaning dishes, or worrying about hydro and electric bills.

That shit, as sexist as it would sound, was woman's work.

He had more important things to do.

"Will you get back in your fucking head?" Viper said. "I want to make it home to my wife and kid. You're making so much noise the birds are getting distracted."

They were flat out on a roof. The building beneath them was abandoned but would give them a perfect vantage point.

Their target?

One of the heads of a ring specializing in trafficking women.

Boss had a real beef when it came to trafficked women and children, so when the price was right, he was more than happy to make the kill. There were a lot of things Xavier knew about Boss and respected him for. If only the bastard would hand over everything he knew about his sister.

What he didn't get was Boss's conflicting interests when it came to women. He had women who worked at Killer of Kings.

Xavier had seen them. Deadly little women who didn't look like they could harm a fly and yet he'd seen how evil they could be. With Boss though, there were the women that he killed, women that he fucked, and then civilian women that he suggested needed to be protected.

"What's Boss's issue with this guy?" he asked.

"It's not our place to question why we do certain things. We get the job done and move on," said Viper.

"I know what getting the job done means, asshole. Don't you ever get curious?"

"I do about a minute each night before I go to bed when I can think about all the shit Boss makes me do. After that, I wait for the next call, and hope my kids don't ever find out what I do."

"I don't know how you can have kids."

"Again, El Diablo, I don't give a fuck what you think. We all make a life from it. Boss gives us the opportunity to do our best work."

Xavier snorted. "We're not fucking artists."

"Nah, we're worse. We paint the streets in blood and watch other people pick up the pieces. I have no illusion that the place I'll end up in is hell. I've got too many kills to think otherwise."

"You believe in that shit?"

"I believe that when we die, it's not the end of us. That we move on to another place. My wife, she's the good part of everything. The light to my darkness. She'll be in heaven."

"But you'll be in hell?" Xavier asked.

"I'll be where I need to be. I know what kind of man I am." Viper glanced toward him. "What kind of man are you? Are you even trustworthy? I know Boss has given you his vote, but I know who you are. You've been loyal to nothing and no one your entire life. You'd probably turn on all of us for the right paycheck."

Xavier stared at Viper.

When he was younger, Viper wouldn't have been wrong.

Growing up with nothing, he had no problem stabbing friends in the back to get what he wanted. They were in a dog eat dog world, and there was nothing anyone could do to save you. His mother sold them like dogs. His sister was taken from him, and he hadn't seen her since. He knew how cruel the world was. A part of him hoped she'd been killed. That someone had the mercy to put a bullet in her brain so she would never know true pain.

That was his biggest fear—that his sister had lived a life similar to his.

The only thing that drove him in this world was his thirst for vengeance. To find the men that took his sister. To make them all pay.

He'd been one of the best locators in the world. He could find anyone, but his sister evaded him at every turn. Even with the breadcrumbs Boss had given him, she was still an enigma.

There was almost nothing he knew.

No way of finding her.

Boss had managed to get hold of information such as her port of entry and her alias. That information was his reason for joining Killer of Kings. But he needed more. Even if she was dead, he wanted to know the truth.

He'd be able to pay his respects and move on.

"Why did you agree to this assignment?" Xavier asked, smirking.

He didn't care that little Viper didn't like him.

Being liked in this world never helped anyone.

Viper shook his head. "You're a fucking idiot if you think any of us has a choice in this. Boss tells us what to do, and we do it. I could be at home right now. Setting up a nice barbeque. My wife marinating some steaks. Instead I'm baking my balls off, waiting for this piece of shit to show up so I can blow his brains out. I have no desire to be here, but this is the price I have to pay."

Xavier shrugged, watching through his lens. The apartment they were staking was impressive, even for his standards. It was spacious, and he saw the kitchen from his position—all top of the range gadgets that screamed money.

This was what he didn't get. Crime wasn't supposed to pay, and yet he'd taken down more rich criminals than he liked to think about.

The real truth was that crime paid the bills.

You got a couple hundred grand waiting for a cop to turn a blind eye, they'd take it. Businessmen were the same.

It sickened Xavier, especially as he'd been one of them. The temptation of money when he'd been poor had been too strong to turn down. It meant power and security.

He was no better than those pieces of shit, which was why he never looked in the mirror anymore.

There was a time he'd look into his eyes and remember the horrors he'd experienced. That drove him to keep on going. To make sure he never suffered at another's hands again.

Only, as time went on, he came to see that the more he looked in his eyes, the more he realized he hated himself. He fucking hated what he saw.

The real monster was staring right back at him.

"We've got movement." Tilting his lens, he saw six men enter the apartment.

There was a woman. She wore nothing, and for some reason he wondered why no one had stopped them. Her hands were bound, tape covered her mouth, and her face was bruised.

Xavier focused the lens as they moved to the apartment. The man, their hit, threw her across the room. With her hands bound, she crashed onto the table.

The men burst out laughing. One man pulled out a gun and fired, the glass table shattering. The broken glass cut her body as she dropped down.

"Wait for it," Viper said. "We need a clear shot so we can take them all out."

He was happy to wait.

Fucking cowards, beating the shit out of a bound woman. It hit too close to home. He envisioned his sister being tossed around like garbage, no one to defend her. She'd be about that woman's age now.

"I counted six," Viper said.

They only had visual on four.

Xavier was starting to get a little fucking irritated.

One of the men lifted her head up, slapped her face and then used his booted foot to crush her into the glass. He could imagine her screams.

Another man kicked her.

He'd had enough.

"Where the fuck are you going?"

He crawled toward the door. Once he was clear, he got to his feet and charged down the stairs. He didn't give a fuck that this wasn't Boss's order.

This was not how he did business. Rushing across the road, he entered the apartment block. On the stairs, he saw one guard who was playing with a ball. All it took was a blade to the neck to kill the fucker. Before he could make a noise with his fall, Xavier lowered him gently on the ground. Taking the steps two at a time, he heard Viper growling in his ear, but he ignored that.

With his knives in his hands, he saw another man just outside of the door to the apartment. The other one they couldn't get a visual on.

He'd checked out the entire layout of the two places.

With the next guard also dead, he leaned the body back against the wall.

"When I say, start shooting," Xavier said.

"What the fuck are you talking about?"

"Trust me." Taking a deep breath, he thought about his sister. "Shoot!"

He kicked the door in, taking them by surprise.

Bullets shattered the glass of the windows.

He rushed up to the first man and attacked him with his knives. Bullets rushed past him, and he used the big guy's body as a shield, moving his way deeper into the apartment.

Withdrawing his knives, he cut the second man's throat, and then the guy he'd seen abusing the woman from above, he cut the bastard's balls off, then sliced the guy's throat, blood spraying out onto Xavier's shirt.

Turning around in the space, he saw glass everywhere, and all the men were down.

"Xavier, get out of there."

"The girl?" He looked at the broken glass table.

"They slit her throat, Xavier."

He saw the blood pooling beneath her.

He was too late.

Once again, he'd failed.

"You can answer to Boss."

****

Alesha woke up with a start.

Blinking the sleep from her eyes, she frowned as she heard the noise again. Something was moving downstairs.

The sound of banging and glass breaking drew her out from the bed. Wearing a pair of pajamas, she was in no way suited to deal with a potential intruder. Xavier said she would be safe here. Grabbing the baseball bat that she took with her to every place she stayed, she opened her bedroom door.

This was the first time an intruder had invaded her home.

Xavier's home.

Not her home.

She only worked here. Just a housekeeper. The woman he kept to keep his life in line and perfectly neat. She cooked, cleaned, and ran the errands he asked for.

She was nothing more than a woman that blended into his life like a piece of furniture. Alesha was a couch.

Pain slashed through her at the thought of how little she meant to him. Not that she was supposed to mean anything to him. He was her boss. Nothing more, nothing less.

Getting to the stairs, she winced as they creaked beneath her weight.

When no one jumped out of her and she figured she was safe, she took the steps slowly, bracing herself against what she might face.

What if it was like out of a horror movie and they were wearing a scary mask and wielding a knife that would slash her into a thousand pieces? Or this was only a dream and she was about to be torn to bits by a man with knives for fingers? *Note to self, never ever watch old seventies and eighties horror films before bed.* She hated scary movies so much, but once they were playing, she needed to know what happened next.

Get a grip.

Once she cleared the stairs, she squeezed the bat tighter.

She'd never been good at baseball.

Stepping down the hall, she walked into the dining room where she saw a large shadow. She screamed and swung the bat, hitting something. The intruder didn't stop though. Lifting the bat, she drew it back about to hit him again when he caught the bat and pulled it from her grip.

Before she knew what was happening, the intruder tugged her into his arms, holding her still. She screamed and fought with all of her might, but whoever had her knew what they were doing.

She couldn't go anywhere.

He was so strong.

She was going to die.

She didn't want to die.

There was still so much for her to do. Become a mother, a wife, know what really good sex was like.

"Will you fucking stop wriggling, woman? You're going to hurt yourself or me or both of us."

She froze.

That was Xavier's voice.

Her boss.

Oh shit.

"That's right. You're hitting your fucking boss and all I was doing was grabbing a drink. If I let you go, promise you won't try any of your deadly moves?"

She nodded. No longer struggling. There was no way she could use words right now.

What if she'd killed her boss? What if he sued her?

He paid her a good wage but not enough to take him on in court. Would she need a good lawyer? It would be bad enough losing this job.

Xavier flicked on the light.

She blinked a few times to get accustomed to the sudden brightness. When she did, she froze into place.

Xavier wore a white shirt and a pair of black pants. His feet were bare.

He held a bottle of whiskey in one hand.

He'd only been holding her with *one arm*?

The bat she'd been using for her attack lay on the ground at his feet.

"Fuck, is that how you greet every man that enters this house?" he asked.

She glanced down at her body and quickly crossed her arms over her chest.

"Nice tits. You don't need to hide them. It's not like I haven't seen it all before. Believe me, there's not much in this world I haven't seen."

His talk about her breasts was not what had her frozen in place.

The blood on his shirt was the reason. That and the scars she'd caught a glimpse of.

His back was to her right now as he poured some ice into a glass then added the whiskey.

Still rooted in place, she watched as he lifted the glass to his lips. "Want one?"

She shook her head. Words failed her. What was she to say?

"I've had a really fucking shitty day, Ashley."

She frowned. "Alesha."

"What?"

"My name's Alesha, not Ashley."

He started laughing, and she wondered if she'd said the wrong thing. Should you correct a crazy person who was drinking? She remembered her days working in bars and needing to watch her words around drunks.

They always made her nervous.

He finished off his drink and poured another one. "Need to numb the pain."

"You're hurt?"

"Nah, I'm not hurt. Just … pissed off. I fucking hate men."

She frowned.

"They're all a bunch of fucking pigs. They think they can take what they want. Hurt women. Pisses me off." He finished the drink and then poured another. "You know, there was a time I didn't care. Women were to be used. A nice pair of tits, a cute ass, three holes to use. That's how easy it was. Didn't want to hear them talk. Wanted to hear them scream and moan. Simple. Easy."

She was somewhat aroused and offended. This wasn't good.

"Then I had to go and remember *her*. My sister. To think about those monsters. Those fucking pigs that hurt women. That take. That rape. That hurt. I can't do that, and I will do everything to help. I didn't help today."

"Did someone hurt you?"

"This blood ain't mine. You don't hit very hard for a girl." He squinted at her and then laughed manically. He was totally wasted. "You know you work for a monster, right? A nasty piece of shit. I've killed so many people."

She swallowed past the lump in her throat.

"Yep, that's me. I'm a taker of lives. So easy to do." He held his hand out and squeezed his fingers together. "Snuffing out life is so easy. So easy."

He kept repeating the word *easy*, and the way he looked, she didn't think for a second it was easy for him.

"I kill, Ashley."

She wasn't going to correct him this time.

If he was thinking about killing, the last thing she wanted was for him to kill her.

She didn't want to die.

He drank another glass of whiskey. How many was that now?

She didn't take a step back.

He was a killer. He had blood on his clothes, and rather than run, she wanted to give him a hug. When morning came, if she was still alive, she was going to have her head examined.

Biting her lip, she watched him, realizing she wasn't afraid. She should be.

"I mean, they were hurting her today and laughing. Who laughs when you crush a woman's face into glass? It's not good. It's not clean. She was just a slip of a thing. Hadn't been fed and they just killed her. Boss was so angry." He pressed a finger to his lips. "Don't tell anyone but I'm part of a secret group." His lips pursed together. "Yep, top secret group of assassins. Boss is our boss." He started to laugh. "Tells us who to kill and when. I've been a bad boy. I shouldn't be drinking. I shouldn't be telling you this." He let out a burp. "I don't feel so great."

There at her feet, she watched as Xavier passed out on the floor, the glass rolling out of his hand. Ice soaked the floor.

What the hell had she just witnessed?

Running away and telling the cops seemed like the right thing to do. Going to her knees, she lifted up his head, and checked his pulse. She didn't want the cops to come.

Whoever this man was, he didn't need the cops; he needed some serious help.

Chapter Three

Everything was dark.

A man groaned.

It took him a while to realize the sounds were coming from him, and his eyes were closed. His defenses immediately kicked in, and he shot up in the bed.

His head ached, and the light hurt his eyes. Bits and pieces slowly came back. He'd gotten drunk. No, fucking wasted.

Back in Colombia, when he'd ruled some of the worst gangs, he attributed much of his success to the fact he never touched the shit he dealt. No drugs. No alcohol. It had been the downfall of so many others.

Last night he'd broken his own rule and had drunk way too much. It was a stupid move in his line of work, where a sharp mind was essential for survival. He scrubbed his hands over his face.

He remembered more. The girl with the slit throat. The guilt. Boss raking him over the coals for not following protocol. The blood soaking his shirt. Xavier looked down, moving the comforter aside. He was only wearing his boxer briefs. He remembered nothing after…

Fucking shit.

He bolted from the bed, nearly tripping in the blankets. *Alesha.* He couldn't remember much, but she was there last night. What had he said? What had she seen?

"You better take it easy. You got a nasty bump on the head."

He turned, completely off his game. Alesha sat on a chair near his dresser. "What are you doing here?"

"I live here."

"I mean *here*. In my bedroom."

"Do you remember anything from last night?" she

asked.

"Not much. Except the fact I should never have stopped at the liquor store on the way home." He massaged his temple, the throbbing growing stronger.

"Yeah, I got the sense you weren't used to drinking."

"Did anything else happen?" he asked with caution. Xavier hoped she'd caught him passed out or mumbling incoherent gibberish.

"Like what? The part where you said you liked my tits or the part where you said you killed for a living?"

Motherfucker.

He began to pace the room, back and forth, back and forth. Alesha was fucking innocent, and because of his stupidity, he'd have to put a bullet in her head. What more had he said? All he knew was that it was too much. Boss would never condone this breach of security. He was already on Boss's shit list from last night.

Now he understood the danger of having a civilian working for him. One slip up and he had to clean up his mess.

But he'd promised to keep her safe.

"I'm sorry for whatever I said. You know, when guys drink they say stupid shit."

"So, you're not a killer working for a secret group of assassins?"

He scoffed, forcing a laugh. "That's a good one. I must have a better imagination than I realized. Too many late-night movies."

"And the blood on your clothes?"

He patted his chest. "Did you undress me, Alesha?"

"I didn't have much choice. You knocked yourself out on the floor. I dragged you to bed, took off the bloody clothes, and washed you the best I could. You've slept like a baby all night."

"How long have you been sitting there?"

"I told you. All night. I wanted to be sure you woke up okay. Some drunks die choking on their own vomit. I heard some horror stories when I waitressed."

He cringed. "Trust me, the drinking part, that'll never happen again. I've learned my lesson."

"I'd offer you coffee, but I know you won't drink it."

He'd never allowed himself to overthink his feelings for Alesha. His life was fast-paced, and she was his housekeeper. Xavier didn't do romance or commitment. And nice girls like Alesha were destined for stable men who could provide the whole white picket fence deal. All El Diablo was good for was killing. "You know a lot about me, don't you?"

"You kept talking about a sister."

His entire body tensed. Graciella had always been his one weakness. She stole his focus, and brought out the worst in him. His desperation to find her had taken over his life. "I have no sister," he said, trying to back up his argument that everything he'd said last night was bullshit.

"So, everything was a lie? The woman you said they killed never existed? That's a really big imagination you have."

"Crazy, eh?" He walked over to the dresser, supporting his weight on his hands as he leaned in close to examine his face in the mirror. "I look like shit."

He usually kept his shoulder-length hair in a short ponytail. Now it was loose and wild, his eyes red-rimmed. What he needed was a long, cold shower.

Staying in bed to recover wasn't in the cards. Boss had an assignment for him today. A punishment for fucking up yesterday. That woman dying on his watch was punishment enough, but he was being sent on a recon mission. Boss knew they bored the fuck out of him.

It was a black-tie event, some fancy fundraiser. Xavier couldn't stand those rich snobs, and he had to force a smile and mingle with them all night long. And he needed a date.

His thoughts shifted to Alesha again. Was this a game they were playing, or did she believe all the lies he was dishing? His hope was to brush this major lapse in judgment off as nothing so he didn't have to kill her. He didn't want to kill her. Imagining those pretty blue eyes permanently closed made him bristle.

"You look good considering," she said, catching his attention. He glanced sideways at her. "You didn't tell me about the blood."

He internally groaned. "It was a crazy night," he said, his frustration growing. "I don't remember much. Must have gotten a cut or something."

She stood up, approaching him at the dresser. Alesha shifted him to face her, then ran her fingertips down his chest. It surprised him how good her touch felt. He thought he'd lost all sensation decades ago. "No, not a single scratch. I would have noticed last night. You're pretty heavy too, by the way. Not very easy to lug to bed."

Xavier grabbed her wrist, her fingers still lingering on his skin. She let out a barely audible gasp. "I work hard, but I play hard, too. Sometimes things get a little crazy with all the booze and bitches. I'm sure it'll come back to me, but I guarantee you won't want the details."

She needed to move on and forget everything she'd seen or heard. He had to push her away. If she kept focusing on things he couldn't explain to her, it would leave him with only one choice. And he didn't want to go there.

"Right. None of my business."

He released her hand. "I know it's a work day, but considering you were up all night because of me, I want you to get some sleep."

"I'll be fine."

Xavier shook his head. She looked exhausted. "No, you're going to sleep. End of discussion."

She headed to the door of his bedroom, and he exhaled in relief. Maybe everything would turn out fine, and she'd move on, never mentioning this shit again. This was the first and last time he drank himself sick.

He wasted no time getting into his en-suite shower, savoring the cool water washing over his face. If only it could wash away his guilt. He was only a few seconds too late yesterday. If he'd known that fucker was going to slit that girl's throat, he could have done things differently. If only he'd listened to Viper and waited before acting.

If only...

He couldn't undo the past. Xavier slammed the heel of his hand against the tiles, over and over until a web of cracks appeared. He wanted to cry, but that dam had dried up decades ago. This was fucking ridiculous. Xavier knew better than to let his emotions get the better of him. His job as a hitman was perfect as it required being numb, heartless, ready to go to hell and back for a kill. It had never been an issue, but that woman yesterday had reminded him of Graciella.

He recalled when he'd freed Chains's woman from being trapped in his basement last year. Any time he discovered an innocent woman being abused, it sparked that weakness inside him, that protective instinct he couldn't seem to shake.

Then his thoughts drifted to Alesha. He could avoid the truth, but he knew damn well he'd hired her because of his attraction to her. Her innocence had pulled him in, and those curves had sealed the deal. It's not like anything could ever happen between them, but he'd hired her nonetheless. Now he'd put them in an uncomfortable position. A dangerous one.

Did she believe his stories?

He'd have to be sure.

His acting skills would determine if she lived or died. But he'd be a hypocrite if he killed her, no better than the piece of shit who slit that woman's throat. Maybe this could be his own test. It was time to put memories of his sister to rest. He needed to rid himself of his weaknesses.

****

Alesha twisted amongst her blankets, the cool fabric rubbing against her freshly shaved legs. She couldn't believe she'd actually fallen asleep with so much on her mind. Now she felt rested and her level head had returned.

That wasn't such a good thing.

She began to replay the events in her head, over and over, trying to make sense of everything. Xavier had been her boss for a few months now, and she'd never had a single issue until last night, so it wasn't a pattern. She wanted to believe he'd just screwed up and drunk too much. And had a crazy imagination. But she knew better.

After dragging him to bed, stripping him, and washing his chest, she'd done some snooping. His wallet had numerous IDs for multiple aliases. His back was scarred, and not from a few childhood mishaps, but deep lashes that had left permanent grooves on his skin. Xavier Moreno wasn't your average man. His crazy story about murder and mayhem was starting to sound more plausible.

But if she didn't believe what he'd told her this morning, the alternative was too scary to contemplate. She wanted to keep her job, wanted everything to stay on the status quo. Alesha decided it would be best to keep her mouth shut. Even though he'd never brought women home, he claimed to be a playboy who partied hard. It made sense, even if she didn't want to believe it.

She opened her eyes, the sunset giving her bedroom a wash of pink. How would she face him again?

Her peripheral vision noticed the slightest movement. She clutched her blankets and looked toward her door. It was open, and Xavier leaned against the doorframe.

"Where's my gun?" he asked, his tone clipped.

"What?"

"I was wearing a harness last night. You undressed me."

She wiggled up to lean against her headboard, her blankets up to her neck. Alesha licked her lips. "I put it away for safekeeping."

There was no way she'd leave the loaded weapon lying around when he was drunk. What if he'd woken up in a rage and tried to use it against her?

He crossed his arms across his chest, raising an eyebrow. "Do you plan on giving it back to me?"

"Y-yes. I'll just get dressed first. How long have you been standing there?"

He ignored her question. "And the clothes I was wearing?"

"They're in my bathtub soaking. I'm hoping I can scrub the bloodstains out. I have a few tricks I can try."

He strode into her room without asking, pushing open her en-suite bathroom door. She heard him draining the water from the tub, then he came out with the bag from her garbage can, his wet clothes in it. "They're not salvageable."

"I didn't even try yet."

Xavier didn't look like the man she'd seen last night. That man had been broken, lost, torn down the middle. Now he was showered, confident, the same boss she'd seen every day since being hired. Could alcohol mess up a person to that degree, or was there some truth in the things he'd said yesterday?

What did he do for a living to afford this mansion?

Why the weird hours?

She'd never questioned anything about him or his lifestyle before, but now her imagination was on overdrive, her mind trying to piece so many things together. Maybe he wasn't a reclusive businessman. Maybe he *did* work for a secret group of assassins. Alesha almost laughed out loud at her own ridiculous thoughts. If anything, he was probably just a dirty businessman.

He stared at her, his knuckles holding the bag of wet clothing turning white. His intensity made her nipples pebble. God, the man was gorgeous. Why wasn't he speaking?

"What size are you?"

She frowned. "Excuse me?"

"Dress size. Shoe size. What are they?"

Her hackles went down slightly. At least he wasn't making fun of her weight. She gave him the numbers, expecting him to grimace, but he didn't. "Why do you need them? For a uniform?"

"I'm taking you out with me tonight. Fine dining. We leave in two hours."

What the hell is going on? She ran a hand through

her hair, the blanket falling to her waist. His eyes darted to her chest, and her cheeks instantly flushed. She needed to get thicker pajamas. "I don't understand."

Xavier stepped closer to her bed. He only wore dark gray joggers and a fitted black tank top. He worked out like a fiend every day after coming home, usually for hours. She could hear the heavy weights clang and his fists making contact with a punching bag. That was all she could decipher since she wasn't permitted in the basement.

He sat on the edge of her bed, and her pussy instantly clenched. She squeezed her thighs together, trying not to focus on the broadness of his bare shoulders, the hardness of his biceps, or the dark ink on his skin. It didn't help that she'd had her hands all over him last night while he was unconscious. She kept telling herself she was just nursing him, doing her job, but that was a total lie.

This was way too much for her handle. What was he doing to her? Their proximity crossed too many boundaries to count. And she didn't care.

"You understand more than you let on, don't you, Alesha?" He reached out with his free hand and drew a line across the seam of her lips with his finger. "I'm not sure if I can trust you."

She said nothing, spellbound by his touch and not sure if she should be afraid of his words.

"I have a business dinner tonight, and I don't feel comfortable leaving you alone just yet. Since I need a date, it's going to work out just fine."

"I haven't done anything wrong. If this is about last night, I was only trying to help."

Why wouldn't he trust her alone in the house? She was his housekeeper. It was her job to keep things together while he was away.

"Yes, my curious little lamb." He stood up, walking towards the door. "You probably don't realize that this house and property are wired from top to bottom. The very best in high-tech surveillance."

She swallowed hard, not liking where this was going. What had he seen her do? Was she in trouble? Did he watch her going through his wallet?

He turned around once reaching the door. "I'll have your outfit here within the hour. Let's call tonight a test of your loyalty, Alesha."

"What does that mean?" she whispered.

"Reputation is everything in my business. I can't have one person tarnishing everything I've worked hard for because of a misunderstanding. That's all last night was—a misunderstanding."

She should have kept her big mouth shut, but it had a mind of its own. "So, you've never killed a person?"

"Have you?"

Talking to him was like pulling teeth. She should be trying to mend all these broken bridges, agreeing that it was a misunderstanding. But, deep down, she'd felt the sincerity when he spoke last night, even if drunk. He was raw, honest, real. Now, completely sober, she had the growing feeling he was trying to cover up the truth.

"Sorry, silly question, I guess." She slipped off the bed with the blanket securely around her body. "I'll get your gun."

He watched her every move as she bent down in front of her dresser and slid open the bottom drawer where she kept her bras and panties. One of her undergarments hooked on the barrel of the gun, and she rushed to pluck it off as she lifted the entire harness out of the drawer. She handed it to him, and he tossed it over his shoulder.

"Where are we going tonight?" Was this a real date? Did he really not trust her alone in his house now? This wasn't looking good for her cushy new job.

"Black-tie fundraiser. I hate them," he said. "Maybe it'll be bearable with you there."

"Misery loves company?"

"Something like that," he said.

"Why didn't you invite one of your flings from last night?"

Alesha wasn't exactly arm candy. And her jealousy had been brewing since he'd told her about his bitches and partying. He tilted her chin up, and she didn't pull away. "If I'm going to pretend I'm with my fiancée, I want to take a woman I'd choose myself. Much more convincing."

"So, we're acting?"

"It's a couples only event, and I need to portray a certain image if I want to blend in."

"And blending in is good?"

"I should say *fitting in* is more appropriate. We won't be blending in once you're wearing the dress I've picked out for you."

Chapter Four

Xavier regretted the dress the moment she walked downstairs toward him. After he'd ordered her an outfit he'd debated on going with the plain black cocktail dress that molded to her curves, showing off a great deal of cleavage, or the red number. The model had a similar figure to Alesha and he'd wanted to see her in the flesh in a dress. Big mistake on his part.

She looked sexy as fucking sin.

The dress molded to her body and flared out at her hips. There were two slits up either side of the dress showing a tantalizing view of leg. The heels she wore made him want to do nothing more than to spread her wide, and fuck her hard.

He'd been avoiding her since this morning, giving her time to sleep.

If she gave anything away about their conversation last night, he'd have no choice but to kill her. Boss wouldn't allow her to live.

She was a loose end.

"Do I look okay for the job?"

Her dirty-blonde hair cascaded around her in loose ringlets.

She looked stunning, and he had no doubt she'd fit in tonight. The aim was to blend. To look like they were one of the rich and elite. Not an assassin and his housekeeper. It was quite funny now that he thought about it.

"You look like you'll do."

He watched the smile fade away.

"All you've got to do tonight is stay on my arm. Smile, don't talk. If someone talks to you, pretend you don't hear them or understand them."

"That seems rude."

"Are you going to be difficult?"

"I'm not going to be rude. It's simple as that. If a person talks to me, I'll talk back."

"You're in no position to tell me what you're going to do. Be careful." He stepped up close to her. Damn, she even smelled good, sweet and tempting. It was going to take a lot of effort to feign disinterest.

She rolled her eyes. "Please, if you were going to kill me, you'd have done it already."

"What makes you think I won't?"

"I don't know. Maybe because after all you revealed to me last night as part of your so-called imagination, I never called the cops or the mental asylum. I'm still here, and I spent hours caring for you and cleaning the blood out of your clothes. I think that warrants not being killed." She pushed some hair out of her face.

Her hand trembled, giving her away. She was nervous, even as she tried to hide it, and he hated that he was the cause. Alesha was never supposed to be part of this.

"You can't tell people who we are."

"I have no intention of doing anything. I don't even want to go to this thing. Don't you have women who you can use for this? I'm not a black-tie event person."

"No. You'll do." He grabbed her arm, moving her toward the door.

"You better stop manhandling me. You're not being fair, and I bruise easily."

He loosened his hold just a little but didn't let her go.

She would be safer with him.

If Boss even suspected a thing, the bastard would kill her.

Leaving his home, he secured all the locks and opened the car door for her.

"Thank you."

He waited for her to get inside. The dress fell open, revealing an expanse of leg, and fuck, he wanted her again.

With the door closed, he moved toward the driver's side. Tonight wasn't about creating waves. Boss gave him simple instructions.

Recon.

Check out a potential crime lord.

The black tie they were going to was a front for trafficking women and kids. Boss wanted a look on the inside and to check out the layout of the house. If Xavier saw anything, he wasn't to react, only take note.

This was going to be hard for him. Women were a weakness. Especially women who were in danger. He had an instinct to protect them, and yesterday's events were fresh in his mind.

"So, we're supposed to be engaged?"

"It's all fake, remember that," he said.

"I'm not going to forget. Don't you need this to look authentic though?"

"What do you mean?" he asked, navigating the roads.

"We're engaged. That means there has to be a ring. I don't have a ring."

He held the wheel with one hand, and reached into his jacket pocket. "Already done." He held it out to her. "Here you go." He'd picked up the simple ring to use as a prop.

"Do you think it'll fit?"

"It better. We don't have time to get you another ring."

She took the ring, and he glanced over at her,

watching as she slid it onto her finger. "It fits. Really well. It's pretty."

Alesha rested her hands on her thighs, and seeing the ring on her finger, it looked good. It looked like it was in the right place. He felt guilty for not picking out something even nicer. Alesha deserved something that had meaning to it, not just a prop. Still, this would do the job.

"What else are we doing tonight?"

"Mingling. Don't start conversations, just laugh at the appropriate times. I expect you to look at me adoringly and to pretend that you're in love with me."

"Wow, you didn't tell me that before you forced me out here."

"We're engaged. It's a given."

"I'm not an actress. I can't pretend like this, Xavier. What you're asking for is too much."

"I've seen the way you've checked me out when you think I'm not looking. You don't love me, but you certainly want to fuck me. When you look at me, just imagine you want to fuck me and I'll deal with the rest."

"You're a fucking asshole," she said, her arms folded.

"Do you want to deny it?"

"I'm not going to do or say anything. You don't have to point it out. Wow, now I feel like the loser housemaid that has the hots for her boss. How are you going to look at me? Or do you plan to be the guy that has one woman on his arm while looking for another to screw with?" she asked.

"Simple. I'm going to be looking at you like I'm hungry for you. How one taste will never be enough and if I didn't have to attend the stupid event, I'd be balls deep inside you."

"You don't mean that."

"Don't I? It's funny because the moment you came downstairs, I could think of doing anything else."

His honesty silenced her. *Good.*

"In all seriousness, I think you should pick someone else."

"I don't have time. If you don't handle tonight well, you can kiss your job goodbye."

"Why? I've done nothing wrong. I helped you. Remember last night when you couldn't even get into bed?"

He still couldn't believe she'd helped him to his room. She must have some strength inside her even if he didn't see it. Earlier he'd planned to keep her in the dark, but he saw the glint in her eyes. She knew too much. The girl was smart and probably a much better actress than she gave herself credit for. No point hiding things when they could get ugly fast.

"You want to know the truth? You're a liability. I should never have hired you in the first place. I didn't need a cleaner. I could keep that place in perfect condition without you. I happened to like your smile, and I figured it would be fun to have a woman around the house. Big mistake on my part. Now if the wrong guy finds out who you are, you're dead. Do you understand me? Fucking dead. So tonight you're going to play the part of loving fiancée and you're not going to get into any trouble. When I tell you what to do, you'll do it. No questions asked. You want to live, you'll do it."

"So much for imagination. Everything you told me last night was the truth, wasn't it? You're a killer." She turned away from him, her fingers fidgeting. He never answered her.

When he pulled up outside of the event, he hoped she was ready to look at him as if he was the only guy in her world. Boss would surely kill her, and if he didn't, well, there's no telling what that son of a bitch would do.

No one really knew the owner of Killer of Kings. Xavier had tried to look into Boss's past and had come up with nothing. There was no record of him anywhere. He'd tried using Maurice, the Killer of King's tech expert and genius, but again, he found nothing.

The world didn't know there was a devil that lived among them.

He didn't even know if Boss was a good guy or a bad one.

Either way, he wouldn't test him. Not right now. Not after one big fuck up already.

Besides, if anyone could find any details on his sister, it would be Boss. He kept tempting him, dangling tidbits of information just out of reach.

After nearly an hour's drive, Xavier pulled up behind a long line of cars. They were four cars away from the door.

"We're almost up," he said.

"I see."

"You can do this, Alesha. I have every faith in you."

"Of course. It's a piece of cake, right? Just pretend I love a monster and that he's not going to kill me if I don't do this right." She took a deep breath. "I should have left you on the floor to sleep. Maybe you would have died in your vomit."

Xavier growled as he climbed out, handing the valet his keys. "Keep her in pristine condition."

Another of the valets went to open the passenger door, but he slid in front.

"No one touches my woman." Taking her hand, he helped her out of the car. "Show time."

****

Sipping on the glass of champagne, Alesha tried

not to think too hard about Xavier's arm around her waist. His hand was on her hip, and she was very much aware of his touch.

"Don't drink too much."

"Yes, Daddy."

"If I was your dad, you'd be over my knee right now having the spanking of your life."

That shouldn't turn her on.

Nope, she wouldn't think about being over his knee, his large hand coming down over her bare ass.

What the hell was wrong with her?

She kept replaying events over and over from the past few months, realizing that Xavier being a criminal made perfect sense in hindsight. This was some kind of dangerous stakeout. The perfect job just had to be too good to be true.

Finishing her first glass of champagne, she put the empty glass on a passing waiter's tray. No one had approached them yet, which she was thankful for. What the hell was she supposed to do? Her nerves were going crazy.

The ballroom was full of wealth, the women dressed in designer clothes, laughing and hanging off men's arms. They all looked like they fit in. Right now, she'd love nothing more than to sit back at home with a cup of steaming hot cocoa and a good book.

Instead, she kept looking at Xavier, hoping people thought she was in love.

She blew out a breath she didn't even realize she was holding.

"Calm down."

"I can't. I expect someone to come out, you know? To start shooting at us."

"All you need to do is relax. Blend in."

"If someone asks you any questions do you even

know what you're going to say?"

Xavier smirked. "We'll just have to see, won't we?"

She had hoped they'd stay in their little corner where no one spoke to them. He had other ideas. She wanted to cry out as they began to mingle with the crowd.

Alesha didn't even know why she doubted his skill.

He knew how to work the crowd. The moment they stopped, questions came at them left and right. She couldn't help but tense up as she waited for Xavier to say something, anything. She should have known he had a plan. He told them his company specialized in technology and he repeated some name and details that clearly impressed some of the men. The women were also looking at him as if he was a piece of meat. She practically believed him herself, he was that convincing.

She placed a hand on his chest. "Let's dance," she said.

"Excuse me. My fiancée would love to dance." He took her hand, leading her onto the dance floor.

Alesha stared over his shoulder, not wanting to look him in the eye.

"You're going to pretend I don't exist?"

"I don't know if I like you right now?" she said.

"Let me know when you decide." His hand lowered to her ass, and she hated how that action aroused her.

He was a killer.

An assassin.

Not someone she should want in her bed.

"You already had a story?"

"That's what I'm paid to do. Anyone here who looks up my name and company will see an entire back story. I have a fiancée and those details are not known, and now I've got you."

"Why isn't your fiancée known?" she asked.

"I had to find someone. I can't exactly pick out just any woman. It's dangerous work."

"I'm your cleaner. Why do this to me?"

"It's fun to see you squirm."

She wanted to hit him but refrained from doing so. As crazy as this all was, she still hoped she had a job tomorrow morning. "Well, you've picked me to play the part, so do you plan on telling me more about what's going on? Are you really a killer? Are we in danger?"

"I can't wait until I can get you alone."

"You're my boss."

He shrugged. "You think that matters to someone like me?"

Twice he'd said something sexual to her. And he hadn't answered her questions. It didn't matter. She knew the truth.

Staring into his eyes, he was focused on her until something caught his attention behind her.

She looked behind her and saw nothing.

"What is it?"

"I just saw a kid. She looked … dirty."

"Xavier, there's nothing there."

"Someone grabbed her."

He was talking crazy. There was no one behind her. "You're only supposed to do recon, remember?"

"I don't give a flying fuck. I'm going to find out what's going on. Stay here." He released her, and she had no choice but to watch him go.

Great.

Now what would she do?

She was tempted to follow him but worried she'd get lost and he'd end up in some kind of danger.

She wasn't trained for this. As much as she wished he'd chosen another woman, she was glad he'd picked her. Xavier was a playboy. He'd said so himself. But she still had a sliver of hope that he felt something more for her.

Leaving the dance floor, she made her way to the corner of the ballroom. People mingled.

The waiter stopped by her and she smiled at him as she took another flute of champagne. Xavier left her and now she was going to drink until she stopped feeling afraid. Sipping the clear liquid, the bubbles tickled her nose. She watched, waiting, and wasn't sure how much time was passing.

Every now and then she expected a large bang or gunfire.

Get a grip, Alesha.

"Now, who is the fool that would leave a beautiful rose, such as yourself, unattended?"

She turned to see a man with long, blond hair that was tied back into a ponytail. His suit and the way he commanded himself screamed money.

"He had to go to the bathroom to take a business call," she said.

"Ah, business. The good old plague that ruins all fun."

"I'm doing okay."

She forced a smile.

Her hands were shaking, and she crossed one over her stomach as she held the glass tightly, hoping she didn't shatter it. She didn't want to talk and say the wrong thing.

"Would you mind if I stand with you?"

"By all means." *No, leave me alone.*

"It is quite a get together, isn't it?"

"It's something," she said.

"All that money and wealth. They're all plotting and scheming how to get more. No one is ever satisfied in this day and age. Always wanting more. Always fighting."

"You seem to take issue with that?"

"Not at all. I own this house," he said.

"Oh."

"The name's Dixon."

"Alesha," she said, pressing her lips together. She didn't know if Xavier had given her a different name earlier. *Shit.*

Nerves got the better of her, the bodice of her dress feeling too tight as she struggled for breath.

Dixon held out his hand, and against her better judgment, she took it, giving his hand a shake.

"It's a pleasure to meet you," she said.

"No, no, the pleasure is all mine."

Pulling her hand back, she was aware of his stare. Intense. Focused only on her.

"Have I seen you before?" he asked.

Turning her attention to him, she shook her head. "No. I spend most of my time with Xavier. He likes to keep me close."

"But will leave you at a time like this." He tutted.

"I know work will always come first." *Please, Xavier, come and save me.*

"How about I entertain you? Come. We'll enjoy a dance."

Every single part of her screamed no, but she couldn't do that. She had to play along and not make waves.

"Sure, what could it hurt?"

I'm going to die a slow and painful death, and it's going to be all of Xavier's fault.

I'll haunt you, Xavier.

Dixon took her hand and she placed her champagne flute on the table as they passed. Within seconds his arms were around her. She put her hands on his shoulders, hoping she wasn't fucking this up.

"You're Xavier's fiancée?"

"Yes."

"How long have you been engaged?"

"A year … I think."

"That's a long engagement."

"He likes to keep me waiting."

"I thought I read in the paper that you've been engaged only four months."

Great!

"That's when he wanted to tell the press." She shrugged. "We had a fight, and I guess he felt the only way to make it up to me was to put a ring on my finger."

I can't take much more.

Xavier.

She wanted to burst into tears. Her heart pounded against her ribcage. Did this man hear it? Did he sense how scared she was? How nervous? A wave of nausea swept over her.

All she wanted to do was to go and curl in bed and pretend there was no such thing as bad men and assassins.

"How do you like the ocean?" Dixon asked.

"The ocean?" Had she missed some of the conversation in her panic? "It's okay, I guess. Lots of water."

"I have a yacht. If you ever want to go out to sea, take in the waves and the views, I'd love to have you. Of course, without your fiancé around."

She chuckled. Was she being hit on?

"Excuse me," Xavier said. "Thank you for keeping an eye on my woman. I'll take it from here." His deep voice dripped of confidence.

"Ah, the elusive Xavier Moreno. You really do have a rare gem in this one. One of a kind."

"It's why I got engaged."

"And a long engagement it is proving to be. We must do lunch sometime, and of course, bring your fiancée with you." Dixon kissed her hand. "Until next time."

As soon as he disappeared into the crowd, she whirled on Xavier. "Don't ever leave me again," she said.

He draped his arms around her hips. "I got what I needed."

"And what's that?" she asked.

"An invite to lunch."

"You wanted Dixon?"

"Yes. He's the one I was doing recon on, and it looks like he as a soft spot for my fiancée."

Chapter Five

He'd called Boss to fill him in on the situation. As soon as he mentioned the mark had his eyes on Xavier's date, Boss wanted him to use her as bait. He should have expected as much. His boring assignment was turning into much more, but it wasn't supposed to involve Alesha. He'd brought her along because his only options were leaving her alone at home to call the cops or tying her up in his basement.

Xavier had given her a bullshit story about women and partying hard. The truth was much darker than she could ever imagine. Not to mention he hadn't fucked around with another woman since hiring Alesha. She confused him. And because of his drinking binge, he'd fucked everything up.

"You only said I had to come along to *this* event."

"Well, things just changed," he said.

She held onto the lapels of his suit jacket, looking up at him with those big blue eyes. He'd done a lot of bad shit in his life, but right now, he wished he'd never hired her. Never introduced her into his wicked world.

"If you expect me to keep playing along, you have to be honest with me. I don't know what the hell's going on, and it scares me. You scare me."

He shook his head. "I'd never hurt you, Alesha." The sincerity in his own voice surprised him.

"Will you talk to me? *Really* talk to me? No lies."

"Not here."

"Fine. What about the little girl?" she asked.

"Gone." The truth was there was no little girl. Xavier swore he'd seen his baby sister, wearing the same filthy dress she'd worn the day he'd lost her, but it was only another figment of his imagination. He was fucking losing it.

"Okay. How much longer are we staying?" she asked.

He wasn't about to tell her he was stalling. Xavier enjoyed having his hands on her much more than he should. He'd fucked everything—young, old, rich, poor. Not a single woman he'd slept with over the years had meant a thing to him. All disposable. His little cleaner with the heart of gold awoke something dormant inside him. He was still deciding if that was a good or bad thing.

"We have to make this convincing first."

"How?"

"I should probably kiss you. Show everyone here how in love we are—including Dixon."

Where was this jealousy coming from? It began eating away at him from the inside out the moment he saw that fucker's hands on her. He wasn't a jealous man.

She swallowed hard. "Okay, if you say so."

"Brace yourself, sweetheart. I'll have to do this my way." He reached down and grabbed one of her ass cheeks, bringing her tight to his body. With his free hand, he cupped behind her head and kissed her hard on the mouth. He expected her to go stiff, to fight him every step of the way. But she melted against him, reaching her arms around his neck as she kissed him back.

The entire world went away. The darkness. The fucked-up memories that kept him up at night.

It was just her.

And the kiss.

When he pulled away, sounds were muted, his vision tunneled. If he didn't know better, he'd swear he was drugged. How else could he explain his deep-seated claim over Alesha? He'd always been attracted to her, but finding out she'd dragged him to bed, taken care of him, and sat with him all night long, changed everything.

No one had ever given a shit about him, not even his own family. He'd been disposable, unwanted, garbage. Being of any importance to another human being … it was addictive.

"I think that worked," she whispered, touching her mouth.

"Yeah, I think it did." Was he fucking speechless? What was he doing?

He'd been trying his best to keep aloof since revealing his secrets. He hoped to push her away, make her hate him so they could keep a distant work relationship—one where he didn't have to kill her. He knew he was pulling at straws. Alesha hadn't exactly acted how he imagined she would. He didn't know what the hell she'd do.

Now what?

Could he keep her? He wanted her, wanted to own her. He'd been denied everything in his life until he learned to take what he wanted, regardless of the cost. But it had always been about *things*—money, power, guns, property. Personal relationships were where he drew the line. He'd been burned too many times, enough to stop caring, to stop feeling.

Alesha would turn out like all the others, like his mother, like the gangbangers who'd taken his innocence. He couldn't risk being vulnerable, giving his heart to a woman.

But there had been something there, some spark between them when they kissed.

He pulled himself together, taking Alesha's hand and leading her to the main entrance. Like every other day of his life, he was on guard, taking in his surroundings as they walked through the mingling guests. He trusted no one, and was never naïve enough to think he was safe.

"Are we going home?"

"Yeah, why?"

"I haven't prepared dinner, and we didn't stay to eat," she said.

He waved his hand once outside, requesting his car from one of the valets. "Then I'll take you out to eat. It's too late to start cooking, and it would be a shame not to see you in that dress for a couple more hours."

Her cheeks flushed pink. It looked good on her. He imagined she'd look just like that after fucking her for half the night. Xavier pushed his thoughts away, blaming his raging hard-on on going too long without sex.

They drove toward the city center. He kept replaying the events over in his head, trying to remember all the details for their upcoming lunch. He hoped Boss gave him the all clear to put a bullet in Dixon's brain. Xavier was already imagining it with vivid detail.

By now, Boss would already have figured out Alesha was his housekeeper. Had he gotten Maurice to hack his surveillance at home? Did he know Xavier got wasted and spilled his guts to a civilian? He hoped that gem was off the radar. When Boss told him to use Alesha to his advantage, he didn't see a problem using her as bait. He'd be there the whole time and trusted his own abilities. But what if Boss wanted her exterminated after the mission? He wouldn't be able to follow that order.

"…your family."

He snapped back into reality, checking the street signs to ground himself. "Sorry, I didn't catch that."

"You said you don't have a sister, but what about your parents? Do they live near you?"

He ground his teeth together. Why was he humoring her? Because she meant something to him— even though he wished he could wipe her from memory at this point. Women always complicated shit.

"Let's not talk about family."

"Xavier, you promised." Her voice sounded young, but then again, she was a lot younger than he was. More than a fucking decade. The pleading tone made him feel compelled to obey her.

He shifted in his seat, his cock uncomfortably heavy. Even her scent had filled the inside of his car, distracting him.

The restaurant was only five minutes up the highway, so he pulled over to the side of the road and put the car into park. "Alesha, why do you have to ask all the difficult questions?"

She tilted her head. "I thought it was a simple question. I'm just trying to start a dialogue."

He unbuckled and turned to face her. Her tits were spilling out the top of her dress, and he had to remind himself to behave and keep his damn hands to himself. Such a sinful body with those innocent doe eyes. He clenched his fist, resting it on the headrest behind her.

"Family is a tough one."

"We're supposed to be honest. No lies, remember?"

He took a deep breath, not used to keeping a promise. "I never knew my father, but that wasn't uncommon in our village. My mother, well, that bitch sold us off to pay her debts. Just handed over her son and daughter, turned the other way, and started fresh. Do you realize what they do to little girls who're taken? You think I'd sell my fucking kids to a gang, to anyone? I'd die first." He realized he was shouting, his face only inches from hers.

Xavier pulled back, running a hand through his hair. His heart was racing.

"I'm sorry," she whispered. He looked down, and

her hand was on his thigh.

"Why are you sorry? It's my shit life. It's not your fault."

"I like the real you, even if it's dark and dirty. My mother wasn't a prize either. Once she got remarried, she wished I never existed. I haven't spoken to her since. It's why I've been struggling for so long."

He'd add killing Alesha's bitch mother to his to-do list.

"What about you, Alesha? Would you sell off your kids for the right price? Put yourself before them?"

"I never thought much about being a mother. I mean, I'm twenty-seven and still a virgin." She gasped, slapping her hand over her mouth. "I'm sorry, I—"

He bolted forward and kissed her on the mouth, rough and demanding. Thoroughly. So much volatile energy was already rushing through his veins, and it easily morphed into a passion he'd never known. He wanted to possess her, body and soul. To become one with her. Xavier moved closer in the cramped space, running his free hand up her thigh, pushing her dress up to her hip. He spread her legs open, reaching between them to cup her pussy mound. He could feel the moisture even through her panties. She jolted, gripping his shoulders.

A fucking virgin? He wanted her even more. His claim grew tenfold.

Not once did he stop kissing her, nipping her lips, playing with her tongue. She mewled, holding onto him, letting him take control. He moved down her neck, trailing hot kisses as he went. Her cleavage was luscious. He ran his cheeks against the pillowy softness, his eyes rolling back in his head. When he pulled back, his stubble had left her pale skin reddened.

"Xavier…"

He counted to ten in his head, taming the beast. Alesha wasn't a whore. He wouldn't fuck her in his car, no matter how desperate he was to be inside her. This was all getting way too complicated, and fast.

"Let's rethink this."

"Did I do something wrong?" she asked. Her lips were swollen, her dress still riding high. He adjusted the hem so it covered her thighs again.

"We were talking," he said. "I got distracted. By *you*."

She licked her lips. "And I never got to answer your question," she said. "No, Xavier, I'd never give up my child, no matter the cost."

Alesha knew exactly what to say to get under his skin.

****

Xavier was her boss, but she was also hopelessly falling for him. The vulnerability he'd shown her last night when he was drunk was the real him, the broken side of the man. If she hadn't come downstairs to catch him in his stupor, she'd still think he was a cold, heartless businessman. After last night, she'd become intrigued.

Now she knew there was so much more to Xavier Moreno than money and impossibly good looks. Once again, he'd shown her a glimpse of his pain, a traumatic childhood she couldn't begin to imagine. And there *had* been a sister. The one he'd denied having.

She wouldn't push him, not after humiliating herself and revealing she was still a virgin. That wasn't information she eagerly shared with anyone.

He didn't seem to care, and the passion they shared couldn't have been one-sided. She just hoped to God she wasn't just another number to him. Alesha wanted to heal him, to show him not all women were heartless.

"We should continue our talk later, no?" he asked. He'd moved back into his seat. When he'd first kissed her, he'd practically crawled on top of her, touching and kissing her like a man possessed. His dominant advance overwhelmed her, but she loved it. Craved it. She could still feel the presence of his palm pressing against her pussy, and she wanted him to touch her like that again. When he stopped, she'd only felt disappointment.

"We were just starting to open up. That's a good thing. I have so many questions," she said.

"Like what? More family bullshit?"

"Not really. I was thinking about your wild nights. Am I just another conquest to you?"

He narrowed his eyes, but she saw the corners of his lips twitch. "There aren't any other women, Alesha."

"But you said—"

"Lies. I'm good at lying. I can hide from the world, put on the mask I want people to see."

"Is this another mask?" She reached her hand out to touch his face, but pulled back before making contact. His dark eyes, straight nose, rough stubble, and thick lips … every detail of his face was perfect to her.

"I don't know what this is," he said. "But it feels real."

She adjusted the top of her dress, and his eyes went to her cleavage. He made her feel like the most beautiful woman in the world. There was no denying the hunger in his eyes. "I can't handle being my boss's fling. If that's what this is, please find another woman to be your date tomorrow."

"I said there are no other women. Since you moved into my house, I haven't fucked around. And stop calling me your boss. I have a name."

"Xavier." She pronounced it slowly. He leaned closer.

"You're worried about women, nothing else? You're a fearless little thing, aren't you?" He touched her jaw, dragging one finger along the edge of her face until he reached her chin. He tilted her face up. "And fucking gorgeous."

"Xavier..."

"There it is again. Hearing you say my name, it makes my cock hard."

Holy shit. She loved his no holds barred way of talking. It turned her on, made her desperate for more. When had this happened? What was she becoming?

"You confuse me," she said. Alesha reached out, slipping her hand into his jacket. There it was, his gun. "Do you always carry a weapon?"

"Always."

"Why? Is your life really so dangerous?"

"You have no idea. And now I have to protect you, too," he said.

She pulled her hand back. "Why would I need protecting? I don't understand why anyone would want me dead. I'm a cleaner, nothing more."

"It's my fault. I fucked up." He lost the flirty quality and turned around, squeezing the steering wheel. "I'm supposed to use you as bait during Dixon's lunch tomorrow, and I will if that means closing this contract for my boss."

"Great. I'm just bait to you." She crossed her arms over her chest, facing forward, wondering why she ever thought there could be something between her and some hired gun. She'd be lucky if she got out of this nightmare in one piece.

"Alesha, look at me," he said. Why did his voice have to be so deep and rough, sex for her ears? She wanted to ignore him, but peeked to her side.

"What?" she snapped.

"Dixon isn't a good man. He's into a lot of bad shit, and doesn't deserve to be breathing. I only agreed to my boss's request to use you tomorrow because I'll be there by your side the entire time." He forced her to look at him, holding the side of her face. "I'll never let anyone hurt you. No matter what. Do you understand what I'm saying?"

She narrowed her eyes. "You've already told me you're the best liar. Why should I believe you?"

"If you were anyone else, I'd already have killed you. Witnesses have a very short shelf life in this game, and my Boss hates loose ends like little girls who know too much."

She swallowed hard, feeling a mix of emotions from being flattered, deeply aroused, to insulted. Something was wrong with her head.

"I'm not a little girl," she whispered.

"You're twenty-seven. I'm not old enough to be your father, but not by much. I'm still trying to understand what it is about you that has me second guessing everything."

She had a laundry list of questions for Xavier. Was he a hired gun? How many people had he killed? Who did he work for? She wondered if a cold-blooded killer like him was even capable of love.

Instead of asking any of her questions, she only wanted to prove that she was woman enough for him. One moment he couldn't keep his hands to himself, the next pushing her away. He confused her, but she couldn't deny she was inexplicably drawn to him.

"Twenty-seven isn't a child."

"No, you're very much a woman, aren't you, Alesha? What do you think I should do? Do the right thing and cut you loose, or be a bastard and keep you for myself?"

Her heart pounded in her chest, her womb coiling tight. "Like a toy?"

"No, just mine to keep." She watched his lips as he spoke. His dark eyes gave nothing away. As much as she wanted him to tell her everything reassuring, everything she craved to hear, she wouldn't beg.

She raised an eyebrow. "Do I have any say in this decision of yours?"

"You can't force a person to love you, trust me, I know. Honestly, if I were you, I'd tell me to go fuck myself. Maybe you should."

"Good thing for you, you're not me."

He leaned back in his seat, crossing his arms behind his head. "Alesha, I'm not a good man. You're looking for something in me you'll never find. I'm a monster, and you deserve better."

"Don't say that. There's good in everyone, and I've seen another side of you. Yesterday. Today. I can see under all your masks. You're not fooling me."

"So, tell me, what do you see? You've seen it all last night. My tattoos, my scars, my demons. That doesn't scare you?"

She smiled, reaching out to grab his tie, pulling him closer. Alesha felt empowered, emboldened, and a little in love. "You don't scare me, Xavier. I've seen the real you, and I like him. Maybe too much."

"Be careful." He combed his fingers into the hair and the base of her neck, then squeezed his fingers into a fist. She whined as he tightened his hold, her lips parting. God, she felt like she'd spontaneously orgasm at any second. He leaned close, so close she could feel the heat from his skin. His lips ever so lightly brushed hers, but he didn't kiss her, leaving her yearning for more. "There are other sides of me you might not like so much."

Chapter Six

"I hate restaurants," Alesha said, taking Xavier by surprise.

Not that he'd consider this all day and night diner a restaurant but he didn't mind it at all.

"You want to go somewhere else?" he asked.

"Oh, no, I'm just saying. I mean, I'm not big on the whole eating dinner while floating on the ocean deal."

He stared at her, a little confused. The burger he was eating his way through tasted like grease. It was the best he could do, and he wasn't about to stink up his car with takeout food.

"What are you talking about?" he asked.

"The thing tomorrow. The boat assassin thing."

"Okay, first off, don't ever say that in a crowded room. This is top secret."

"Fine. Fine. Wow, I get it. Don't say anything." She rolled her eyes, and he found that to be the cutest thing.

It was strange how he found things to be cute with Alesha but annoying as hell with other women. The fact she didn't cringe away from him in fear intrigued him.

"You do realize the kind of danger you're in, right?"

She sighed. "Let's see, the kind of danger I'm in? Yeah, I know. I saw your array of … memorabilia. You know the kind that goes bang." Her eyes were wide, and he saw she was trying to speak in code.

Laughing, he shook his head, and picked up another fry.

"Does this mean we're not going to that guy's boat tomorrow?"

"It's a yacht, and no, it does mean we're going."

He saw her lips pout. "I hate boats."

"You know that can be kind of insulting."

"What?"

"It's not a damn boat."

She rolled her eyes. "Can we get off the boat thing? I don't like it. I don't want any part in this. I didn't even want to be your date for this thing tonight, and you didn't even feed me good food."

"I fed you."

"Yeah, and you're going to feed me to the wolves," she said.

It was the last thing he wanted to do.

If he'd not royally fucked up and Boss wasn't breathing down his neck, he wouldn't even opt for this as a suggestion.

"The last thing I want to do is put you in danger."

"But you're going to. It's fine. I mean, I want to help. I do." He watched as she released a sigh. "I'm just a cleaner. A housemaid. I don't know what you want or need from me."

"First, you're going to need to look the part."

"More clothes?"

"You could sound excited about it. It's clothes. Don't all women love that kind of stuff?"

"I'm not like all women." She wrinkled her nose. "So, what's the play?"

"The play?"

"You know. The mission. What do we do? How do we do it? Who are we playing?" she asked, looking excited.

"This isn't a game."

Another eyeroll. "I get that it's not a game, but I've got to figure this out. I can't be like other people and just let things roll and what not. I'm not designed that way."

"You don't need to worry about a thing. The less you know, the better."

"This guy though, you want to use me as bait, and I don't want to mess this up for you."

Xavier saw the real concern and care in her eyes. Why couldn't she be different? Why did she have to make him feel like this? He didn't want to take her on that damn boat—no, yacht. He wanted to keep her safe, and the only way to do that was to keep her far away from the monsters that surrounded them.

He knew the real world, and no one in it, not even him, deserved someone like Alesha.

"I won't let anything happen to you."

"Xavier, I'm not a fool. I know how this works. You're going to need me to distract him while you go and search all around his … place. I don't mind. Whatever I can do to help. I'm involved now, so there's no going back for me. I accept that, but I don't want anything to happen to you." She pressed her lips together.

Taking her hand, he turned it over so that he could look at her palm. So pale. Running his thumb across her pulse, he felt it beating rapidly. "You'll be a distraction, and for that reason I can't give you any more details. We're together. You're my fiancée, and we're hitting a hard patch."

She laughed. "Wow, our engagement isn't going to last, is it?"

"Everyone hits a few snags. You've just got to be your charming self. Seems Dixon already has a hard-on for you."

"And if he tries anything? What do you want me to do?"

"What would you do? Tell me what Alesha

would do. You weren't acting tonight, which is why he was drawn to you. Don't play a part. Be yourself and we'll get this. We'll make it work."

"You always sound so confident. I don't have the first clue what I'm doing."

"You do." He brought her hand to his lips, kissing her pulse.

He heard her slight gasp, and he released her hand. This was a bad idea. He shouldn't be kissing her, touching her.

She was a virgin. Since she let that little detail spill just a few short hours ago, he couldn't bring himself to concentrate. He wanted to be the one to bring her pleasure. To show her what it was like to take on a real man.

His dick ached, and he didn't want to think about Boss and the threat he posed.

He wanted Alesha, no doubt about it.

How could he have her all to himself without Boss interfering? He didn't want to fuck up his place at Killer of Kings after working hard to prove himself the past year.

Boss had eyes everywhere, so Xavier had to be careful. Especially, if he was still able to help find his sister. Boss was close to giving him more information on his sister, he could feel it.

Running his fingers through his hair, he waited for her to finish her food. The moment she did, he pulled out a couple of notes, leaving a generous tip, and took her out of the diner.

Helping her into the car, he waited for her to strap in before getting seated. Gripping the steering wheel tightly, no matter what he tried to think, he couldn't think of a reason or an excuse to keep Alesha breathing and in his life. How had he gotten himself into this mess?

"Apart from when you abandoned me to go and snoop and I was talking with a guy that scared me, I really enjoyed tonight." She smoothed out her dress.

He turned to look at her. "You did?"

"It's the first time I've dressed up in a long time. I liked it." She rested her head on his shoulder. "Thank you, Xavier. Tonight, I actually felt like a princess."

All he was thinking about were the many ways that he could take her as his own. She was thanking him for a nice night, and he wanted more, so much more. For the first time he was thinking about the future, his own happiness, one woman.

Gritting his teeth, he drove the rest of the way, pushing his foot to the gas. He had to get her home. He needed the safety of his house to be able to do what he wanted to do next.

Without saying another word and with her head on his shoulder, he drove as safely as he could.

She was really getting to him, and he couldn't control this need that bubbled up inside him. Parking up in his secure garage, he placed all the necessary codes before exiting the vehicle. Helping Alesha out of her side of the car, he put a hand at the small of her back, and headed toward the main door.

"Do you think we're being watched even here?" she asked.

He hoped not.

"Stop worrying about everything."

Stepping over the threshold, he kept hold of her arm, closed the door, keyed in the code, and then pressed her up against the wall.

"I don't like this dress," he said.

"You were the one that picked it out. I thought we'd gone over all this dress talk."

He put his hands on her hips, sliding them up so

she had no choice but to lift her hands above her head.

"What are you doing?" she asked.

"What I started earlier." He brought his lips down on hers, needing another kiss. Another taste wouldn't hurt him. He could turn off his emotions whenever he chose.

His cock hardened, and as he pressed himself against her soft body, he couldn't help but become addicted. Locking his fingers with hers above their heads, he held her steady against the wall.

There was no escape for either of them.

Keeping both of her hands in place with one hand, he ran his other down her body, touching her tits, feeling the hard bud of her nipple against his palm. When he stroked a finger back and forth over that peak, she released a little moan, and he swallowed her cries. She was becoming his obsession.

He couldn't get enough.

One kiss. One taste. It was never going to be enough, not for him.

"I need to have you," he said, breaking from the kiss

"Please, Xavier."

"Tell me you don't want this."

"I do. Touch me again."

Sliding a hand between her thighs, he cupped her pussy. He slipped beneath the fabric, teasing her slit through her panties, knowing he wouldn't enter her cunt. When the time came to take her cherry, he wanted her to be on a bed, legs spread so that he could hold her down and enjoy it. He wasn't certain, but confident Alesha was the only virgin he'd tangled with.

She let out another gasp as he played with her clit, pinching the sensitive nub between his fingers, enjoying her cries. Her moans echoed around his hallway, and they were the best sounds a woman could make.

With just a few more strokes against her clit, and she was coming, screaming his name, begging him not to stop. It wasn't hard to comply. Even as she came and he watched the orgasm wash over her body, he didn't want to stop.

He let go of her hand and she attacked his pants, sliding open the belt, but then as she got to the zipper, his cell phone rang.

They both groaned.

"Ignore it," she said.

He pulled out his cell phone and saw who it was.

Boss was calling. There was no way he could ignore this.

"I can't," he said.

"Please, Xavier."

This was business, and she was all pleasure. So long as he kept Boss happy, he'd be able to keep her alive.

"Go and get a shower. I've got to take this. An early night will have you well rested for tomorrow." He accepted the call. "What's up?" he asked, staring into her eyes.

If she spoke now, there was a risk to her life. He hoped she wasn't fool enough to try this.

There was only so much he could do to protect her, to save her.

Boss was his own personal army.

She shook her head and left the room, her disappointment palpable.

The scent of her pussy still lingered on his fingers as he talked to Boss. He closed his eyes, leaning against the front door.

This woman was messing with his head, and he

had to do right by her. There was no way he could allow anything to happen, not to Alesha. Even when he tried to turn off his emotions, they were still there. She was the real deal.

****

It was official.

Alesha hated boats.

They were all the same, be it yacht or cruise ship.

It was a boat on the ocean. Glancing down at the water, she wondered if there were any killer sharks, or big giant sea creatures that were going to eat her. Keeping her sunglasses on, she tried not to think about the dangers that surrounded her everywhere. This was the ocean. Besides all the big bad monsters lurking beneath the ocean depths, there was also the added risk of drowning as well. That would suck.

Drowning was one of the scariest ways to go, in her opinion.

She didn't want to drown. Why had she never learned how to swim?

"I can't believe your fiancé keeps leaving you unattended," Dixon said, coming to join her. Her body tensed as he drew closer.

"Yeah, well, considering he loves bo-yachts, his stomach doesn't agree with him." She pressed her lips together. Xavier had warned her plenty of times on the way over to the docks to not call it a boat. *Yacht, yacht, yacht.*

Tomato, *tomato*, whichever way people said it.

"His loss is certainly my gain." Dixon held two drinks in his hands.

She'd always been told to never take a drink from a stranger, and here she was, living on the edge. One day cleaner, the next seductress. What was next?

He offered her a glass, and she took it without

question. Keeping a hold of it, she looked over the railing into the water, dark and sloshing against the sides of the boat.

"Penny for your thoughts," he said.

"I was actually wondering if there were any sharks in the water." She forced a smile. Xavier had told her to be herself, and she didn't have the capabilities to flirt even just a little bit. Not after last night. Not after he'd brought her to orgasm only to send her to her room like a little child.

"There have been shark sightings around. I myself like to sit and watch them. I feed them as well."

"Isn't that dangerous?" she asked.

"Only if you're sinking and you become the bait."

"Ha, wow, that is so funny." She laughed, thinking about her own baiting predicament.

She kept trying to think of things to say or do that wouldn't show him just how nervous she was.

"You act like you've never been on a yacht before."

"It's true. I can't deny it."

"But Xavier owns plenty of them."

She rolled her eyes. "Of course, he does. It's all part of the image. I don't like to, you know, do stuff like this. I prefer to keep my feet firmly on the ground. I'm a simple woman that likes the simple things in life."

It was very true. She liked having a roof over her head, cooking, cleaning, washing, making sure Xavier didn't vomit and choke on it. Of course, never in her wildest dreams did she think she would actually be babysitting a killer. That was just so far out of her comfort zone, but she also didn't imagine getting fondled by him either, or being used as bait. Her life had changed so dramatically in the past forty-eight hours she was struggling to keep up. She checked around the deck to see if Xavier was anywhere in sight. He'd given her the excuse that he needed to use the bathroom.

She didn't have a clue what that actually meant in code, only that it had to mean something. He was an assassin.

Try to remember that little tidbit of information when his mouth and hands are on you.

"It's what makes you a rare find, Alesha. You're not dazzled by this life. I can see that."

I'm really kind of scared of you actually.

Instead of speaking her mind, she just smiled and tried to listen to what he was saying. As he spoke, she couldn't help but wonder what dark secrets he was hiding. If she didn't know better she'd think he was sincere, but Xavier said he was a monster.

"How about I take you on a tour?" he said.

The last thing she wanted to do was be alone with him. Seeing no other reason to argue, she nodded. "I'd love to."

He placed a hand at her back, and she cringed. She had opted out of a bikini and instead settled for a bathing suit with a sarong around her waist. Xavier had told her there was no other option for her to wear, and of course, most of the women on board wore bikinis.

"Do you know everyone here?" she asked.

"I do. Most of them are gold-diggers. They're always around anyone with money."

"You're used to it?"

"It comes with the territory. When you have money, people want it and are willing to do anything to get it. And I mean anything."

He led her toward the back of the yacht. There were two people making out.

"Come on, there's a lower deck. For some privacy."

Red alert.
Red alert.
Xavier, help!

"Why can't we stay on deck? It's so lovely with all those views."

"You'll get to see the views below deck. Don't worry. There's also an AC. You'll be comfortable, trust me."

Every single part of her was screaming to get away, to run and hide. Instead, she followed him because that was what she was supposed to do. Xavier owed her big time. Not anywhere on her application did it say become bait for a possible kingpin and risk losing her life.

Dixon led her below deck. The stairs were narrow, and the drink she held, she wondered if it was drugged.

Wasn't this what happened to naïve women? They were always drugged after being offered a drink from a stranger.

"Is this your only yacht?" she asked, reminding herself not to call it a boat.

He chuckled. "It would be like asking a billionaire if they only had one set of diamonds."

She laughed. "Of course. Silly of me." Her skin crawled she was so uncomfortable, looking side to side and feeling twitchier by the second.

"Your man has certainly kept you protected."

"It's what he likes to do." She pushed some hair out of her face.

Stepping below deck, she felt the chill in the air.

She felt too cold but didn't say anything or dare complain.

"Are you not going to take a sip of your drink?" he asked.

"I'm not thirsty. This was a nice thought."

"You sure? One sip? For me?"

She didn't like being put on the spot. Her heart raced. Catching the sight of a fishing book, she gasped. "Ah, so you like to fish?"

"Some, I'm not an expert."

Neither am I, buddy.

"Do you bring other men's fiancée's down here often?" she asked, glancing at him over her shoulder.

He was watching her, and she didn't like how intense he was. Something felt off.

"I have to say you're a first, Alesha."

"I must be special then. I'm shocked. A handsome man like yourself being all alone."

"I've not found the right woman." He kept looking at her, and licked his lips.

Keep flirting. Keep doing whatever you have to do.

"You'll find her."

"What makes you think I'm not looking right at her?" he asked.

This was bad. So very, very bad.

"Dixon, you're really sweet. Honestly, I'm flattered, but I'm engaged and I love him." She didn't like how easy it was to say she loved Xavier. He better be saving the entire freaking planet right now because she was trying not to panic.

Dixon didn't take the hint that she really didn't want him.

He took a step toward her. She held her breath.

"I have often wondered what it would be like to find a woman who will like me for myself. Not for the life I can give her, or the money I can lavish her with. A woman who will look at me, see the real man, and like what they see."

He was way too close.

She struggled not to flinch away from his touch as he stroked her cheek.

This was really bad.

She was all alone with a monster. Her days of waitressing came back to her, making her even more uncomfortable.

Xavier wouldn't tell her the full extent of Dixon's crimes, but she had a wild imagination and that was coming into full effect right fucking now.

The backs of his fingers ran down to her pulse, and then he cupped her cheek, his thumb running across her lip.

"This is really inappropriate," she said.

"I think you need to reconsider the man you're going to marry. Every chance he gets he dumps you, leaves you alone. I wouldn't do that to you. You'd be treated as a queen with me."

The space between them was getting less, and his lips were getting scarily bigger. She was panicking.

Her heart raced and not in a good way.

Everything inside her screamed to get away.

Would a woman scream in this instance? Yell at him?

Should she let him kiss her?

Xavier, when I see you, I'm totally kicking you in the balls and you're going to deserve every second of it.

Dixon's lips dropped on hers, and she felt her stomach recoil.

This man was not for her.

Chapter Seven

Alesha stumbled backwards, but Dixon kept her from falling. She hated his hands on her. Hated any man's hands on her—except Xavier's. This charade was proving more than she could handle. With so many gorgeous women to choose from, why was Dixon obsessed with *her*?

The sound of a person tutting came from behind him. Dixon turned to look, and Alesha peeked to the side to see if it was Xavier.

It was a woman.

She was stunning, with long black hair, smooth as glass. Her make-up was done to perfection, her ruby red lips slightly parted.

"Didn't your mother teach you not to take without asking?" she asked.

Dixon scoffed, tossing up his hands. He turned to look at Alesha. "Can you believe this?"

She shrugged.

He turned back around. "I don't remember you from my guest list," he said.

She smiled, but it was almost evil. "Details."

"You need to go." He reached out to grab the woman's arm, but she moved impossibly fast, twisting around and bringing a metallic blade to Dixon's throat from behind.

She whispered in his ear, loud enough for Alesha to hear. "You have a harem of whores. Cut this one loose."

The woman slid the blade along the side of his neck, a single bead of crimson blood escaping down into his collar. Then she twirled around, tucking the blade into a wide black garter on her thigh before leaving up the staircase. How could she move so gracefully in those sinfully high heels?

What the hell was going on?

Just before she disappeared from view, she looked down and made eye contact with Alesha. She froze until the woman was out of sight, then gasped for air, not realizing she'd been holding her breath.

Dixon pulled out his cell phone, talking to his security detail, then put it away. "I'm so sorry about that," he said, blotting his neck with a cloth handkerchief. "The crazies just seem to come out of the woodwork these days."

"Right," she said, not sure what to say. Where was Xavier? "Maybe we should go where there are more people. She could have killed you."

"I'm not afraid of her," said Dixon. "My security team will have her rounded up within minutes."

"Will they throw her overboard?" she asked to lighten the mood.

He laughed. "They should, but no, they'll contact the coast guard and have her arrested."

She nodded. "Good. Someone like that is definitely dangerous. I was too shocked to move."

"I can protect you, Alesha."

She almost scoffed out loud, coughing lightly instead. He couldn't even protect himself from some socialite. Xavier was the only man capable of truly protecting her. Would he kill for her? Right now, he was too busy to think about her safety, but she was bait after all. Did Xavier expect her to go all the way with Dixon? Did she mean nothing to him?

Her mind raced as Dixon crept closer, coming for round two of his unwanted advance. Apparently, that woman's warning had no effect on him. Alesha still couldn't get those dark eyes out of her mind.

"I should check on Xavier." She backed away.

"He's a big boy. I'm sure he can handle that weak stomach of his," he said. "I suggest you keep an open mind. Trust me, one day you'll realize Xavier will never have the stability I can offer."

"What do you do for a living exactly, if you don't mind me asking?" Small talk was better than kissing and touching.

"Imports, exports. I won't bore you with the details."

"And the dinner yesterday? That was for a charity, right?"

"A fundraiser. For the manatees."

She narrowed her eyes. "The manatees?" Alesha walked to the portal windows and peered out, trying to look occupied. Xavier told her the charity dinner was a front for human trafficking. She doubted the manatees benefited from Dixon's little soiree.

"It's good to give back once in a while," he said.

"Sure. Of course."

"Does Xavier involve himself with any charities? I never thought of him as a philanthropist like myself, but I could be wrong."

"Oh, he loves giving. Give here, give there. Whales, seals, manatees. I can't keep up with him." *Oh shit.* She hated these specific questions where she had no answers planned. It was one thing to act like herself, but another to lie on the spot. Quick wit didn't come easy when her nerves were frayed thin.

"You're a good woman caught up in something you can't begin to imagine." He tossed his handkerchief on the bar and backed her up against the porthole. Her entire body tensed. She wanted to tell him to fuck off, but wasn't sure how far Xavier expected her to take this ruse.

He placed a hand on her hip, and all those years of being at the mercy of drunks and perverts when working at bars came rushing back—the helplessness, the shame, and anger. "No, I can't do this." She shoved him away, cursing herself for not keeping to the mission. "I love Xavier."

"Wrong answer," he said. His hand was around her neck the next second, squeezing hard enough to steal her breath. She clawed at his arm with both hands, gasping for air. His eyes were flat, and all traces of the gentleman he'd tried to portray had vanished. "Do you really think you're my type? Did you believe the bullshit lines I fed you?" He chuckled. "Alesha Marie Sanders. It didn't take long for my men to get a full work up on you. Too easy really. Xavier is getting sloppy."

He knew who they were. It was all a trap. Did they have Xavier?

She felt herself drifting away, and she was helpless to fight it. Her vision blurred, the room growing darker. Was she going to die? Would he throw her overboard? Feed her to the sharks? A great shadow appeared behind Dixon, like a demon about to consume him, and an arm came around his neck. The hand around her throat dropped away, and she coughed, air rushing back into her lungs, the room coming alive with color and light.

"Trying to kill my fiancée?" Xavier had Dixon at his mercy. "You're a terrible host. I think we'll have to cancel the rest of our lunch date."

Dixon held onto Xavier's thick bicep, attempting to speak. "We're on my yacht, in the middle of the ocean. Do you realize how many men I have upstairs? They're all aware you work for Killer of Kings."

Killer of Kings? So, Xavier did work for a group of assassins. Everything he'd said when drunk was probably the truth. Alesha was still frozen in place, her hand on her neck.

"What men?" Xavier winked at her, and her heart did a little flutter even under the circumstances. "You're the only one left, Dixon. Did you think my boss would send someone that unprofessional?"

"You used a civilian. I had her ID'd within an hour last night."

"Actually, she's where you went wrong. You should have kept your hands to yourself. I don't like sharing." Then a sickly crack made her stomach roil, and Dixon's lifeless figure fell to the ground in a heap, his head at an unnatural angle. She stared down at the body.

"You broke his neck. Is he dead?"

"I certainly hope so." Xavier stepped over the body as if he'd done this a thousand times. He probably had.

He pulled out his phone, scrolled through his messages as if she hadn't almost died and her entire world wasn't upside down. "Hello?" she said, trying to get his attention.

Xavier didn't look up at her. "There was a woman. What happened?"

"I don't know. She was protecting me, I think." Alesha didn't want them to run into that gorgeous woman. She would be too much of a distraction, and Alesha's confidence was already taking a hit today. "I can't believe you're more worried about her. I could have died, Xavier. Do you realize that? Do you even care at all?"

This time he looked at her, returning his phone to his pocket. He stepped closer, cupped her face with both hands and held eye contact. "I just killed fourteen men, and no one at this luncheon is the wiser. I have you bugged, and heard your conversation with my mark the entire time. I wouldn't have left you alone with him otherwise. As soon as you were in real danger, I was here."

"This is crazy. I thought this was recon?" Her voice trailed off. She wasn't able to process what was happening. Her world consisted of normal people things like grocery shopping, cooking, and worrying about bills. All this death, the chaos was something out of a movie.

"That was yesterday," he said. Xavier's ran his thumb across her cheek, a slow, sensual drag. "I did hear a lot in my earpiece that I wasn't expecting. You *love* me?" He raised an eyebrow.

"I was playing the part. You told me to act."

"No, I told you to be yourself."

"Well, the real me would have kicked him in the nuts for touching me without asking. I was behaving so I didn't ruin your mission."

"Next time follow your instincts. No one's allowed to touch you but me." Xavier tilted her head back, examining her neck. He cursed, lightly touching the sore spots. She'd definitely have bruises tomorrow. "I should have come faster."

"What happens now, Xavier? We're on the ocean. There are dead bodies everywhere. Oh my God." She squeezed her eyes shut. "They'll put you in jail."

"You're too cute." He kissed her on the forehead, no signs of concern on his face. His presence and confidence made her feel safe. "There's nothing to worry about. A walk in the park."

"Everything went so wrong. He said he knew who I was. The real me, not your fake fiancée."

"It went exactly as planned, Alesha. I did what my boss asked, and now it's time to go home."

"Just like that?"

He took her hand, leading her to the stairs to the main deck of the yacht. "Do what I do every night. Turn it off. It's a job, nothing more."

"Easy for you to say."

****

Alesha had showered and gone to bed hours ago. The events of the day had worn on her nerves. Xavier swore she'd fracture into a thousand pieces the way she carried on. He had to remind himself she'd never been subjected to the horrors he'd lived through, and murder wasn't a part of her daily routine.

He sat behind his desk in the study, waiting for Maurice to get back on the line. He'd done his time in his gym, venting his frustrations. His feelings for his cleaner were messing with his head. That little part of his brain he so easily turned on and off to avoid feeling emotions was useless when it came to Alesha.

Xavier may have told Alesha everything had gone according to plan, but that was a little white lie. Dixon had found out who Alesha was, which meant others knew. He didn't want her in danger or to be used against him. All the hitmen at Killer of Kings with women had that extra liability hanging over their heads. He didn't want that responsibility. This lifestyle was his choice, and he didn't want to drag an innocent woman down the same path.

He also couldn't cut her loose, which led him back to his original predicament—he wanted something he couldn't have.

"Facial recognition software," said Maurice. "She applied to be bonded a few years ago for a cleaning job. Once her information's on file, it's easy to hack. They'd just need her picture or fingerprint to pull up the information."

"Okay, we know how they got it. I want to know what they plan to do with it."

"It's anyone's guess," said Maurice. "The information could have died with Dixon. Or they could try to get their hands on Alesha to get back at you for killing their boss."

"Yeah." He rubbed his temple. "This is exactly why I believe hitmen should be bachelors for life."

"Did you break your rules?"

He exhaled. "Maybe. It's complicated." Maurice wasn't exactly his friend, but they did communicate frequently for information exchange. He usually had good advice, but there was only so much Xavier was willing to share because he knew the hacker was loyal to Boss first and foremost. "Did you find out anything on the recording of that woman?"

"She's not in any of my databases."

"Alesha said she had Dixon at her mercy. What the fuck does that mean?"

"There are females in this business, Xavier. You know that. She could have been a hired gun."

"Then why not kill him when she had the chance?"

"Maybe she was there for you."

Xavier scoffed. "If she was any kind of professional, she'd know Alesha was my date and would have used her against me."

"You're right," said Maurice. "Probably just a jilted lover he forgot about. She wanted her piece of revenge and got it."

"If you hear anything else, give me a call."

He put the phone away, and Xavier leaned back in his leather chair, his arms behind his head. Boss didn't let on that he knew anything, but Xavier was certain his boss knew better. When he'd called to give him an update after leaving the yacht, Boss had congratulated him for completing the mission. Xavier had single-handedly taken out Dixon and his closest men. It was what he loved doing most—working with his hands. It beat recon any day.

But the mission wasn't over yet. The trafficking ring went deeper, and Boss had a client willing to pay top dollar to root out the kingpin. Xavier had to team up with Killian and Bain tomorrow. Intel had their target at a factory by the city pier for a meeting in the morning. It was the perfect chance to take them all out. When the entire cell was gone, Alesha wouldn't be in danger.

"You're still up?"

He jolted to an upright position, looking towards his office door. Alesha stood there in a pink robe, hugging herself. "What are you doing here?" he asked.

"I know I'm not supposed to be in this part of the house, especially your office, but I figured things were different now. No need for secrets."

Xavier stood up, forgetting he'd only slipped on a pair of black workout shorts after his shower. Her gaze traveled down the length of his body. The way she looked at him made his cock hard. Why did she have so much control over that appendage?

"This isn't what I want, Alesha. Involving you was a mistake. We should try to go back to the way things were."

"Easy for you to say," she said. "The things I've seen aren't things a person easily forgets."

He stalked closer, hoping to instill a bit of healthy fear into her. "What you saw today was nothing. The things I've done with these hands, you have no fucking idea." He held up his hands to punctuate his warning. "If you could see the things I've seen, you wouldn't be so eager for more."

Xavier whirled around, running a hand through his loose, damp hair.

"Your back." Her hands were on him, smoothing along his skin. He jerked, not used to affection or coddling. If he had to imagine heaven, some place outside the darkness of his own mind, it would be the feel of her touching him. She was gentle. The concern in her voice confused him.

She traced the raised scars on his back, and then her lips kissed along the old wounds. Each burn and slash was a reminder of the hell he'd been through. From ten years old and onward, his life had been a battle. Before that, extreme poverty had stolen his childhood.

"You've seen it before, no?"

"I was more worried getting you to bed and dealing with the blood. What happened to you, Xavier?"

"Let's not get into that," he said. He turned back around and shackled both her wrists to keep her from touching him. "You shouldn't be here."

"Where did you get all these scars?" she asked, not heeding his warning. Alesha was an enigma. His fearless little cleaner. He released one of her hands, and she reached for his neck.

He placed his hand over hers. "You think you want me, but you don't. Trust me on that."

These good girls flocked to bad boys like moths to a flame. Maybe they wanted excitement, domination, or whatever the fuck they didn't get from daddy, but Xavier wasn't a bad boy. He was her worst fucking nightmare. He wouldn't be able to love her, just destroy her.

"You wanted me earlier. Or don't you remember the way you touched me?"

He licked his lips. The scent of her strawberry shampoo, her swollen lips, the yearning in her eyes—she was a big problem.

"More mistakes. I can't even count the number of women I've touched the same way."

She narrowed her eyes and stepped back. "You're

an asshole. I keep thinking there's something there, and then you do a one-eighty."

"Now you're getting it," he said.

"Do you have any feelings left at all?" she asked. Her eyes filled with unshed tears.

"Don't cry for me. I don't deserve your tears."

She shook her head, angrily wiping her eyes with the back of her sleeve. "What is it? You love another woman?"

"I don't love another woman, Alesha. Something's broken in me. Fucked up." He put his hand on his chest, slapping himself a couple times. "There's nothing you can do to fix it."

"So, I'm supposed to believe you feel nothing for me?"

He clenched his jaw down hard. "I feel a lot for you." He took a section of her hair and felt it between his thumb and finger. "I want to fuck you. How do you feel about that, my little virgin?"

She whirled around, dashing for his door, but he grabbed her around the waist and pressed her to the wall.

"Get off me! I hate you!" Hot tears traced down her cheeks.

He held her steady despite her struggling. "I'm sorry," he whispered. "I'm sorry, baby."

The tension in her body eased, her heavy breathing calming. He felt like a bastard, trying to scare her away when every instinct told him to protect her.

"You bring out the worst in me."

"How? I'm not judging you. I'm just trying to understand," she said

"In my world, kindness is a weakness. My boss can sense it like a dog smells shit. I don't want him to hurt you."

She reached up and touched his cheek. "You'll

protect me."

"You give me too much credit, Alesha."

Her fingers trailed along his jaw. "I feel safe with you."

"You shouldn't."

She shrugged. "I just happen to believe that kindness is a strength. And I think people can change, can become better."

Alesha was a light to his darkness, and he wanted more. He may be a bastard for not walking away, but he leaned closer and kissed her on the lips.

Chapter Eight

Part of Alesha wanted to push Xavier away and tell him to not fucking touch her. She was hurt that he kept blowing hot and cold. She had no way of knowing which way was up and down. She didn't do these things with men.

Flirting didn't come naturally to her.

She was used to being overlooked.

No one ever wanting her.

It's why she was the cleaner.

She provided a service that everyone appreciated but no one cared about who did it. She was just a piece of furniture, and yet as his lips touched hers, she didn't want to push him away. She had no wish to fight him or for this magic between them to stop.

And there *was* magic.

She couldn't explain it.

He was a cold-blooded killer. Someone she should be terrified of and yet she couldn't hold herself back or look away from him. Even as her life had been in danger today, she'd worried for him, not for herself. It made no matter what happened to her, but she couldn't think of the world without Xavier being part of it.

After the briefest of kisses, he pulled back. His hands cupped her face, his thumbs stroking her cheeks, and she merely stared into his dark eyes.

"I know you hate me right now."

And that was the truth. She only hated him *right now*, right this second. There was no way in hell that she'd ever be able to hate him for a lifetime. It simply wasn't possible for her. She wanted to protect him. To wipe away the memory of the scars so that the only thing he remembered was the feeling of her, the reminder of her touch. The taste of her kiss.

Damn it.

She was losing her mind, and she couldn't even control it. Xavier was the kind of man she should avoid, but was inexplicably drawn to.

"I don't hate you." She licked her lips, trying to find her voice. Her throat felt incredibly dry as she stared at him. "I could never hate you."

He smirked. It was that knowing smirk that she really didn't like. Why did he have to look so sexy when he did it?

"I just don't like you very much right now."

"But you don't hate me."

"Hate is a strong feeling."

"One you're incapable of, no?"

She didn't respond. There was no point. He'd make of it what he would, and she didn't have the energy to change him or to fight him.

One of his thumbs moved toward her mouth, and he ran it across her lip. "Dixon was a fucking fool."

"Why are you talking about that monster?" Was this another cold moment? She couldn't keep up, and it was messing with her head.

"Because I heard what he said to you. That you're not his type. The only reason you're not his type is because a piece of shit like that couldn't handle a woman like you. He wouldn't know what to do with you if he ever got you in his bed. He was a coward. He preyed on the weak, and he thought you were that. He had no idea of the fire inside you."

"I think you've got the wrong woman here, Xavier. I'm not fire."

He smiled.

A genuine, honest smile.

She swooned.

"He bought and sold women. He's used to them

being terrified or too drugged up to even care what's happening. You're not like that. You were honest and sweet and sexy all wrapped up in one package."

She shook her head. "You're wrong."

Suddenly, he pressed her against the wall. Her back hit it with a thud. His body was flush against hers, and she felt the hard ridge of his cock as it nestled against her stomach.

"You feel that, baby? You feel how I want you? You make me crazy. You think today was easy for me? I've never cared about anyone before. Never wanted to. All I've ever wanted to do is get in, kill, and be done with it. Instead, I had to listen to you talk, to ramble on with Dixon. To many men, your rambling may be a fucking turn-off, but to me, I relish it. I want to hear your thoughts, your fears, all of it. You distracted me and I wanted to hurt Dixon for not paying attention, but above all else, I wanted to torture him for days and weeks, to make him beg for death long before I ever let him have it—because of you. Because he said those vile things to you. You're fucking everything, Alesha. Don't let any man make you think differently."

"Why are you saying these things to me when you were being so mean just a few minutes ago?"

"I'm not a good man." He leaned in close, and she frowned as he seemed to inhale her scent. "I'll never be good. I'm a monster to the core. Always have been. Always will be. I know what death is. I look into its face every single day, and I challenge it. I've been playing with it since I was a little kid, and I offer up my victims willingly. But, it'll never be you. You're too good for a man like me." He stared at her lips, and she heard him groan. "You're driving me crazy. I shouldn't want you. Shouldn't even care that you're right here, right now, mine for the tasting, for the touching."

Before she knew what was happening, his lips were on hers, and she lost all thought. She should push him away.

Tell him to get lost.

To leave her alone.

She couldn't do it.

Even as her hands grabbed his shoulders, preparing herself to push him away, she didn't. She gripped him tightly, begging, hungry, desperate for his touch. His tongue traced across her lips, and she moaned, opening her lips and letting him inside.

She didn't want to push him away.

Part of her was terrified he'd refuse her, insist he wasn't good enough. The more he tried to push her away, the more she wanted him.

Warmth flooded her pussy as his hands moved down her body, one of them sliding down her back to cup her ass. The other tracked to her breast, squeezing her flesh. He rubbed his palm across her nipple, and she arched up, wanting his touch more than anything else in the world.

"Please, please," she said, moaning his name, needing him.

"You're so fucking sexy and beautiful, and you make me want you so damn much. Do you realize that? No woman has ever made me this desperate."

"I want you, Xavier."

"Yes, I know you do."

He pulled at her robe, and it fell open to reveal her modest nightshirt. It had a picture of an ice cream on the front. It was so unsexy it was unreal, but Xavier didn't seem to mind. He tugged the nightshirt up her thighs and his hand lay flat on her stomach.

"Are you wet for me right now?"

"Yes." Her panties were soaked through.

Heat flooded her cheeks as he cupped her between the thighs, his fingers pressing against the fabric of the panties so that they dipped between her slit.

"I feel how wet you are. You want my cock. You want my fingers and my mouth. I really shouldn't have you." He groaned as he kept rubbing. The friction against her clit felt so incredibly good. She saw stars dancing before her eyes, but he didn't let up. Not once.

Please. Please. Don't stop.

She couldn't voice the words, and she hoped he understood what she wanted from him.

"A good man would walk away. A good man wouldn't think about spreading you open on his desk, licking the cream from your pussy and then opening you up, taking your cunt, and filling you with his spunk, but with you, Alesha, I lose all thought and common fucking sense." He released a growl and within a second her panties were tugged from her body. He pushed her legs apart, and his hand was back to stroking her clit.

Only this time there was nothing between his fingers and her body. She was open to him, spread wide, waiting, ready.

Her eyes fluttered and closed as she arched into his touch, and then she cried out as his lips sealed around one of her nipples through her nightshirt. He sucked her through the fabric, then moved onto the next bud. The tug of the fabric seemed to enhance the sensation against her tit, and she cried out with an answering pulse between her thighs.

He made her nipples wet as well as her shirt as he sucked her.

"I need to see you. Take your shirt off."

She didn't need telling twice. Lifting up her immature shirt, she threw it to the floor. She stood before him completely naked, waiting for him to give her the next instruction. She was at his mercy, and she wasn't even afraid. Far from it.

Her lips were dry, and she waited. Xavier raked his eyes over her nude body. She could feel his hunger, and it only increased her desire.

"You have no idea how sexy you are, do you? How you make me feel. I'm rock hard, and it's because of you. Because of what I want to do to you."

"What do you want to do to me?"

"I want to make you forget everything from today and only remember my touch."

She wanted that more than anything. The events of today aren't ones she wanted to remember. Both of his hands touched her waist, and he pulled her away from the wall.

"What are you doing?"

"Taking you to my room."

****

The last thing Xavier should be doing was taking Alesha to his bed to fuck her. He had a complete list of what the right things to do were. The nice things and yet, he didn't want to play by the rules. Whoever that woman was, she could have targeted Alesha. Before he'd even gotten to her today, she could have been dead, and he'd have never known the softness of her body against his.

That wouldn't do. Not for him.

He couldn't allow another second to go by without knowing her touch, memorizing her kisses, and owning her body. The moment he did, he hoped he'd be able to come up with a plan to save her.

Boss couldn't get his hands on her. He wasn't above using a woman to get what he wanted.

Xavier picked her up in his arms and carried her to his bedroom. She didn't fight him, and he suspected that had to do with her naked state and the fact she was so wet for him. So ready.

He wanted to fuck her, to take her, to make her ache for him.

To wipe away the memory of Dixon's touch.

He put her on her feet the moment they were in his room. Cupping her face, he took the kiss he craved, loving the feel of her lips.

"Touch me, Alesha."

She ran her hands up his chest, her touch so light that it was driving him crazy.

He wanted her to score his chest with those nails, to beg him for more, and to demand that he fuck her.

Xavier had to keep on reminding himself that she was a virgin. That she'd never known the taste of a man or experienced what he could give her.

She ran her hand back up his chest, smoothing them over his shoulders.

"I'm done waiting."

Stepping away from her, he pushed down his gym shorts. Next, he got rid of his boxer briefs, not wanting them to trap his dick. Wrapping his fingers around the rock-hard length, he stared at her fuller body. The curves he'd been wanting beneath him. He'd imagined those thick, juicy thighs wrapped around his waist as he drove inside her.

She was an addiction already, and he'd not even had a taste of her.

There's no way he should be hungry for her without even licking her pussy or feeling her tight cunt wrapped around his dick.

Closing the distance between them, he moved her back until her legs hit the bed and she dropped down. He pushed her back, going down with her, taking her lips in a searing kiss. Xavier moved down her body, licking and suckling each nipple without the nightshirt between them.

This time, she cried out. The sound was better than magic, his cock harder than oak.

Her moans echoed off the walls, turning him on even more. He didn't want her to stop. She had huge, gorgeous tits. Soft and perfect. Lavishing each hardened bud, he felt her arch up. Her fingers sank into his hair, holding his head still as he nibbled those tight bundles of nerves.

So addictive.

He couldn't stop the hunger that was consuming him.

"Please," she said, moaning his name.

"Yes, that's it, baby." Pulling out of her touch, he pressed her hands to the bed, stopping her from touching him. "You keep those hands there."

"I want to touch you."

"Soon." He wouldn't be able to last if she touched him. He needed to keep constant control or he was going to lose it.

She kept her hands beside her body, and he kissed his way down her stomach, his tongue dipping into her navel before sliding down to the top of her pussy. Pulling her to the edge of the bed, he spread her legs wide, staring at her slick cunt.

She's still a virgin.

Remember that.

Be careful with her.

Using his finger, he teased across her clit and her back arched. Her cries were sweet music to his ears, and she hadn't even had all of him yet.

Replacing his finger with his tongue, he watched her as he sucked her clit, staring up at her body. One day he was going to have to film her because he wanted to see every single reaction as he licked her pussy. See that need build inside her.

"Oh, Xavier, that feels so good."

Using his teeth, he created a small bite of pain that had her legs opening even wider as if she couldn't get enough of what he was doing to her. He knew *he* couldn't get enough, was hungry for more of her pussy. She'd be his—only his. He'd keep her so satisfied, she'd never want to leave.

"Please, please."

"Do you like my mouth on your pussy?" he asked.

"Yes, please, don't stop."

"You're mine, Alesha. I will never let anything happen to you. Your body, it belongs to me. I own it. You'll do everything I want because you know what I can do for you. I can give you this mind-blowing pleasure." As he talked, he stroked her clit, knowing he was using her own pleasure against her.

The poor little virgin didn't stand a chance.

He didn't think he could survive if anything was to happen to her.

He had to do everything in his power to keep her safe. Other members of the Killer of Kings had found women. They'd somehow found a way to have this life and their loved one all combined together.

Why couldn't he have that?

"Yes, Xavier, I'll do anything. Just please don't stop."

He had no intention of stopping, and even though he'd gotten her submission while he was about to give her a mind-blowing orgasm, he would hold her to it.

The moment he took her, claimed her as his own, it would be the day that her other life ceased to exist. She'd belong to him in every single way.

She'd be his woman.

She'd have his ring on her finger, and he'd make sure she was the happiest woman in the world.

You're talking crazy right now.
What the hell is wrong with you?
You can't keep a woman.
You've still got to find your sister.

He pushed all of those thoughts out of his mind and instead focused on the beautiful woman beneath him. He'd deal with everything else when the time came.

Sucking her clit into his mouth, he used the tip of his tongue to slide back and forth, glancing up her body to watch her come apart.

She was so fucking beautiful, all soft, pale curves and innocence.

Her tits shook and quivered, and he couldn't wait for her to come. He'd make her so wet that he'd be able to fuck her with ease. With him not being a small man, it was going to hurt regardless.

Keeping the lips of her pussy open, he licked, sucked, and teased her clit, drawing her ever close to the edge of her release. He kept her right there at the pinnacle, letting her wait for it, building her arousal, tasting her until he could no longer stand it and wanted her to come.

Hurtling her over the edge, he smashed his face against her pussy, swallowing down her sweet cream as she screamed his name.

The sound echoed off the walls, and he fucking loved it.

Xavier knew he could get used to this and that this one taste wouldn't be enough. How could it? Alesha was everything, and he'd known it the first time he met her. She'd called to a part of his soul that he'd believed was long gone, with his sister.

No, this was more than that.

Alesha called to the monster within, teasing him, taunting him, making him want to come out and play, and fuck did he. So damn much. He couldn't get enough.

He'd had countless women over the years, and they all meant nothing. Commitment was not in the cards for him, not after being sold off by his mother and losing his sister. To say he had issues with women and trust was an understatement. But Alesha, she saw the real him and didn't run away screaming. She wasn't afraid, and the fact she fucking cared was something he'd never experienced.

When she'd hurtled into a second orgasm and her pussy was practically dripping, he pressed a kiss to her clit and helped her exhausted body to move up against the sheets.

"That was incredible. I had no idea it would be like that," she said.

"Good. It's only going to get better." He moved between her thighs, savoring the softness of her skin. She was such a full, curvy woman, so sweet, so open, so innocent.

And all mine.

He'd never been good at sharing.

There was no doubt in his mind that he'd fight Boss for her.

"What is it?" she asked.

"What?"

She gave him that sexy smile that he loved so much. "You're looking at me ... weirdly."

"It's because I'm thinking about taking that cherry of yours. Taking it all for myself."

"You're not taking anything if I'm freely giving it."

"You're giving me your virginity?" She nodded. "Why?"

"Because I want to, Xavier. You mean a lot to me."

He recalled how she'd told Dixon today that she loved him. For a split second he'd been struck dumb by her words. Nobody loved him.

El Diablo, a killer, hadn't known what to do or say because he'd felt hope. Something he'd not felt in so long and didn't even think he'd been capable of such emotion.

This cleaner, his innocent woman, was bringing him to his knees, and he had to be careful. If Boss for even a second got a hint that she meant anything to him, he'd be screwed.

"I've never been granted such a precious gift before."

She reached up and cupped his cheek. "You sound like a man out of the dark ages. It's just my body, Xavier."

"It's a part of you, and it can only be granted once." To him, men who deserved to have that kind of innocence didn't kill people on the weekend or as part of their lives. "I will treasure this, always. You'll own a part of me, Alesha."

"Which part?"

"You already know." He leaned down, claiming her lips, not wanting to let go of her. She was so fucking beautiful, so sweet, his everything. He knew he kept repeating the same things, but he couldn't help but marvel at the pure strength of her.

Spreading her thighs, he gripped his stiff cock, which hadn't lost any of its rigidity while talking to her. It's like his body didn't know how to be turned off by her. Her voice, her smile, every part of her turned him on.

Running the tip up and down her creamy slit, he

got his dick nice and wet, wanting to make this as easy as possible for her. He didn't want to put a condom on, even though he knew he should.

Skin to skin.

Flesh against flesh was what he wanted.

Nothing between them, he held eye contact, moving his cock to her entrance. He wanted to see her as he finally made her his.

Chapter Nine

Alesha gripped the sheets as Xavier pressed the head of his cock into her slick pussy. She'd never been more ready for anything. Her body was practically thrumming for him to rid her of her virginity. It wasn't a sacred possession—even at twenty-seven she'd never found a man worthy of giving it to. Xavier may seem like the worst possible choice, but she saw beneath all the hardened layers. Saw the little boy, the fractured man she'd seen that day when he was drunk. There was so much more to him than appearances alone. And damn did he have the appearances part covered.

His dark hair was loose, coming down to his chin. Those dark eyes reminded her of a panther on the hunt. The five o'clock shadow on his face was rough, and she knew how it felt rubbing between her legs. Alesha stared at his thick lips and the massive shoulders looming over her body. His arms were hard with muscle as he supported his weight on one forearm above her.

"More," she said.

He was going incredibly slow for such a proven bad boy. It turned her on and made her feel special that he was taking the extra time for her, but she honestly didn't need it.

"Take it easy, baby. Let me enjoy this. I want to feel your pussy squeezing the shit out of my cock." He kept moving deeper inside her, slow inch after inch. She felt her walls stretching to accommodate his size. The fullness was overwhelming, shivers skittering along her skin as all her nerves seemed to burst with sexual energy.

She wriggled beneath him, waves of heat and need driving her crazy. Alesha ran her hand through his hair, pushing it off his face. He froze, then leaned down to kiss her. He tucked his arms under her shoulders and lowered the rest of his length between her legs. She groaned into his mouth as he sank in to the hilt.

He kissed her, but it was so much more. She felt their connection solidify, felt his vulnerabilities, his passion, everything he kept under lock and key.

His cock throbbed inside her, but he wouldn't budge.

"Is it mine now? Do I own your cock?"

"You own it. My cock *and* my heart." He ran his lips over her eyes, then pressed his forehead to hers. This was so much more than sex.

"I feel so full," she whispered.

He took a breath, a man on the edge. "Please tell me you've adjusted to having me inside you."

"I'm more than ready for this."

"You have no idea the restraint I'm using right now, baby girl." He pulled out and slowly ground back in, teasing her, making her pussy hungry for more. "You're so tight, so fucking delicious. I want to fuck you hard enough to break this damn bed."

"God, yes. Do it."

He picked up a slow rhythm, sliding in and out, creating enough friction that her body responded, craving so much more. She prodded him with her heels, desperate for what she knew he wanted to really give her. Alesha wasn't a slip of a woman. She could handle Xavier and his big dick.

Wanted his hard fucking.

"You're so wet, so damn juicy." He groaned, picking up the pace. The bed began to shudder, the headboard clapping the wall with each thrust of his hips. He filled her to the hilt over and over again. Each time he pounded against her clit, she climbed higher. "Tell me you love being filled with my cock."

She closed her eyes, another beautiful orgasm

building inside her, stealing her inhibitions.

"Tell me, baby. I want to hear it."

Alesha loved the sound of him talking dirty to her. "I love your cock."

"You're only mine."

"Only yours," she repeated.

"Good girl. This body belongs to me now. Mine to fuck. Mine to protect." He nuzzled her neck, sucking her earlobe. Everything he did screamed experience and skill. She loved every minute being in Xavier's bed. She was ready to commit to him, body and soul. Was he ready to sacrifice in the same way?

"Are you mine?"

He pulled back to look down at her. "You're the only woman for me, Alesha. I'm done fucking around. From now on, I'll be pleasuring you and no one else."

"No more pushing me away. No matter what," she said between breaths.

"Promise."

A week ago, she never would have believed the chain of events that she'd experienced recently. Her hot-as-hell boss with the big bank account turned out to be a hitman for hire. And he fucked like a machine. She'd given him her virginity … and he'd promised a lifetime together in return. Was she being naïve, or was this a match made in heaven?

They kissed, hungry and desperate. She couldn't get enough of him.

Then he took her harder, deeper, his back breaking out in a thin sheen of sweat. He pistoned in and out of her body, all hard-packed muscle and strength.

"Come for me again. Let it all go," he said.

She stopped fighting her release and relaxed her muscles, holding him around the neck. Her orgasm came barreling to the surface, heat and calm flooding her lower stomach. Then she detonated, her hips arching up as she milked Xavier's cock over and over in delicious ripples. She'd been taken to heaven and back in the arms of the devil.

He groaned, holding her tighter to his chest as he followed her, filling her with his essence. The weight of his body briefly came down on her until he supported himself again. When the intensity of their lovemaking settled down, only the sounds of their heavy breathing remained.

Xavier rolled to his side, supporting his head with a hand as he stared at her.

"What?" she asked.

"You look beautiful after sex. Your cheeks are flushed nice and pink. Just as I imagined." He reached out and brushed the stray hairs off her face. She was sweaty, her heart still beating hard.

"Tell me something, Xavier. Do you still feel the same way now that sex is out of the way?"

"Why wouldn't I? I'm not a teenager. I know what I want, and I don't plan to do this once."

She shifted to her side to face him. Alesha traced a fingertip along the ink at his neck. He had to be the sexiest man alive. How could something so good be bad?

"What happens now?"

"I have a quick job to do tomorrow, and then we'll figure things out."

"What kind of job?"

He frowned. "My boss wants me to handle the rest of the crime ring Dixon was involved in. It went higher than him."

"Do you need a date again? I can help." She couldn't help but smile. Although she hadn't been the best actress, it had been thrilling and terrifying in equal parts on the yacht.

"I think I can handle it. I told you I'd protect you, and I plan to keep that promise."

"What if I can help? I'm not afraid, Xavier."

He touched the tip of her nose playfully. "You're fearless, aren't you, baby?"

"Sometimes." She held his wrist, looking at the scars on the top of his hand. "Not always."

"What are you afraid of?"

She shrugged. "Of you getting killed. Losing you before we even get a chance to know each other."

"I know you *very* well, Alesha." He winked, trailing the backs of his fingers along the curve of her breast.

"That's not what I mean." She swatted him playfully.

It didn't take much for her deep-seated fears to rise to the surface. "I'm afraid of you walking out on me." Her mother had done the same, and the thought of it happening again made her feel anxious and alone.

"I'm usually good at that. Getting close with people is something I've always avoided, you know? When you learn from an early age that everyone wants to use you for something, you stop trusting. Stop caring."

She swallowed hard.

"It's different with you, Alesha. You opened my eyes, made me realize how good it feels for someone to give a shit about me."

Alesha intertwined her fingers with his.

"What happened to your hands?"

She felt the wall he kept up growing stronger, but she didn't want their relationship based on secrets or lies. "Old scars."

"It shouldn't take being drunk before you open up to me."

"Where I come from, it's not like here. It would

give you nightmares." He licked his lips, and once again, she wanted to erase the past from his memories. "After my mother sold us off, I lived through years of torture, being forced to do all kinds of shit."

"Xavier…"

"It's okay. I survived. I learned to shut it all out. To forget the pain," he said. "I guess it all hardened me, and I lived for revenge. I've done a lot of evil shit in my life."

"It wasn't your fault."

"You don't have to defend me. I know what I've done. The problem now is getting people to believe I've changed. The men I work with don't trust me, and no matter what you think you feel, you don't trust me either."

"I'm trying my best. I'm still here after everything that's happened. I gave you my virginity."

He smirked. "Yes, you did. A gift I didn't deserve."

She leaned forward and kissed his lips. "We can't change the past, Xavier, but we can make a better future. I'm starting from today."

He tucked her into the crook of his arm as he rolled to his back, his fingers gently caressing behind her neck. Tomorrow he was going to risk his life again. How many days and nights would she have to worry about him coming home alive or not? Alesha's faith in new beginnings may be strong, but a relationship with a hitman would put her to the test.

****

Xavier pulled his collar higher. There was a sharp chill in the air at this time of morning, especially by the water. He stared out beyond the stacked containers on the dock to the distant horizon. No matter how hard he tried to forget the past, it continued to haunt him. He didn't regret the killing, the backstabbing, any of the violence ... because they all had it coming. What he couldn't move on from was the sister he left behind. Was she alive? Dead? Did Boss know more than he let on?

He'd always had that little weakness, a part of him that couldn't stand to see a man abuse a woman. It all stemmed back to her—Graciella. They'd dragged her away, kicking and screaming. He watched his little sister until he could no longer see her. Then his own nightmares began. Since the day they were separated as children, he never knew what became of her. Part of him didn't want to know because it would probably be too much for him to handle. But he had to find her, to apologize for not being able to save her. He was no longer a boy. Nothing on heaven or earth would stop him from saving her today ... or from protecting Alesha.

A foghorn sounded in the distance, snapping him back to the present, and reminding him why he was there.

Xavier made his way to the meeting point. Bain and Killian were supposed to be his partners in this raid. The three of them would be able to take down a damn army. Although he hadn't worked too much with Bain, Killian had been one of the men to train him. Boss had strict guidelines for anyone joining Killer of Kings.

Most of his life, he'd been El Diablo. He had no mercy as he climbed his way to the top of every criminal organization he ever joined. Things were different now. He had no desire to rule Killer of Kings. It started as an information exchange, but now he wanted to be trusted, to become a comrade to the other hitmen. But trust had to be earned. Maybe creating a new life would never be in the cards for him.

He found Killian around the corner of a container, leaning against the metal wall as he checked his clips.

"Morning," Xavier said.

Killian nodded once and continued checking his gun. "You bring coffee?"

Xavier ignored the Irish bastard and dropped his duffel bag. "I brought the big guns."

His peripheral vision caught Bain coming toward them. That motherfucker always looked ready to kill. Had he ever seen him smile?

"Two have arrived. There should be at least one more vehicle on the way. Maurice has eyes all over our location," said Bain.

"Are we taking prisoners?" asked Xavier.

"This is a one-stop hit. The cleaning crew is on standby."

A bloodbath. Xavier could handle that. It was more difficult trying to keep key players alive for interrogation when the guns came out. This should be easy. They had more than enough firepower and experience for the job.

"Yeah, no civilians *this time*," said Killian.

"What's that supposed to mean?" Xavier didn't like his tone or what he was implying.

"Viper told me what happened last week. Damn shame what happened to that girl."

He wanted to put his fist right into Killian's twisted mouth, but kept his cool. He knew Killian had a major soft spot for women. His history was almost as fucked up as Xavier's. But he wouldn't sit by while he called him out on something he never intended to happen.

"I made a judgment call."

"Didn't work so well, did it?"

Xavier's heartrate picked up. He faced the other hitman. "I know you. You would have done the same damn thing."

Killian shrugged. "Maybe. Maybe not. What's in question is you. Can we trust you to play by the book? It would be nice if I could go home to my wife and kids tonight."

"Then leave now, chicken shit. The big boys can handle this without you."

They were face to face now, neither willing to back down.

"Break it up, boys. Another car just pulled in," said Bain.

The tension dissipated as they refocused. Xavier had gotten to know Killian well over the past year during his training. He was a good man, hard and soft in equal parts. Xavier was more pissed off with himself. The memory of that girl getting killed only feet from him still haunted his dreams. But he couldn't go back in time and fix shit.

"Okay, we'll let them get cozy, and then we'll move in."

"Do we need a distraction?" asked Xavier.

"I don't know what you're talking about. We don't need a fucking distraction. We have these." He held up one of his assault rifles.

"There are three of us. It should be a cake walk," said Bain.

Killian adjusted his harness. "Hey, *El Diablo*, there's only one way into that tower. Don't wimp out now."

Bain clapped Killian on the shoulder. "Relax, big boy."

They all looked in the same direction as Bain. A little yellow car was parked in the distance, and a woman walked up the metal stairs to the look-out tower. *Alesha.*

"Who the fuck is that?" asked Killian.

He watched her. His woman. The only good thing

in his life. She'd followed him here, tailed him without him even realizing it. What the fuck was she thinking? How far was he gone that he didn't even realize he was being followed?

"It's my housekeeper."

"Say that again," said Bain.

"Why'd you bring your housekeeper to a firefight? She's going to ruin our element of surprise and get herself killed."

"Shit, she must have tailed me. I'm going in," said Xavier, drawing his Glock and barreling forward. Bain put a palm to his chest to hold him back.

"A lot is at stake," said Bain. "I don't want an innocent woman to get hurt because of me."

Should he confide in these men, tell them Alesha was his woman, tell them he was a lovesick fool? They were all married hitmen, so maybe they'd be able to understand the turbulent emotions boiling inside him right now.

Why did he have to mention this to Alesha? She thought she was Nancy Drew or some shit, not realizing all his assignments were life and death reality.

"Don't worry, she'll be fine," said Killian. "We'll deal with it."

"How?"

"We've done this before. We improvise." Killian paced in the confined space. "Maybe if I shoot her in the leg, it'll get her to the ground before they start firing."

"*No, no, no.* Back to the drawing board," said Xavier.

"Maybe a distraction is a good idea. I can blow up one of the containers." Bain pulled out an explosive device from his jacket.

Killian scowled. "Boss wants this off the radar. No explosions."

"Two of us go in firing, the other shields the girl and gets her out safely. Does that work?" asked Bain.

"Okay. Let's do it," said Xavier.

Every minute waiting and stalling was taking a year off his life. She was up in that room alone with all those pigs. The human trafficking kingpins who wouldn't think twice before hurting Alesha.

She had no clue what she was doing. Had she overheard his conversations last night with Boss and Killian? His little spitfire was going to get herself killed. If they got out of this alive, he'd give her the spanking of her life.

The three of them made their way closer to the building, keeping low, the colored containers as their shields. It was early, no ground crew around yet. The seagulls gathered by the water, their cawing filling the morning air. He held his breath, focusing, knowing he couldn't lose Alesha.

The stairs were grated metal, and the windows in the tower gave a full view of everything from the yard and docks to the stairs they three of them were climbing. It was time for El Diablo to come out and play.

Chapter Ten

Ten hours later

"You actually told her to come help you?" Boss said.

Blood leaked out of Xavier's side, but he didn't care about that. He'd been through worse. It was the woman lying in the bed that matted to him most. Everything that could have gone wrong today, had. He'd never known such a clusterfuck.

He was so tired. Bain and Killian were at his back.

Everything had gone from bad to worse.

Alesha had followed him to his hit, and now she lay unconscious, her body hooked up to a bunch of machines.

"Obviously not. What do you think I am?" Xavier said. Not once had he ever regretted a decision. No mistake had ever been made on his watch because he knew what the fuck he was doing. He always knew what he was doing.

From the time he could remember, dealing with what happens when the shit hits the fan was his thing.

Pressing a hand to the glass, he saw lights and heard the machines beeping.

She'd gotten hurt, shot, and it was all his fault. If he hadn't mentioned his assignment, she still be home safe and sound.

He didn't want her involved. Why did she have to show up?

Boss grabbed him around the throat and pressed the side of his face up against the glass. "You think I didn't know what was happening? That I didn't know how you mouthed off about being part of Killer of Kings? You can't fuck, take a piss, or even shit without me knowing about it. You know why, because I've got enemies that would scare you to fucking death. I know what darkness is. I've looked it in the face too many times. I know my men, and I know the women they stick their dicks into. *You* fucked this up. You think because you're El Diablo that it makes you invincible? Today you let everyone fucking down, and if she dies in there, it's on your head, not on mine."

"Fuck you." He pulled away, attempting to slam his fist against Boss's face. "I didn't do shit."

Boss didn't even care.

He simply grabbed Xavier's wrist, twisted it, and he had no choice but to drop to his knees or his wrist would have been snapped.

"You're a little boy, Xavier. A little boy looking for his sister. You're nothing. You had one job to do, and you couldn't even do that." Boss looked at him with disgust, letting him go. "Get him the fuck out of here."

"I'm not going anywhere. I'm not leaving Alesha. You owe me, Boss. I've been working for you almost a year, and I still don't have my sister back."

"I owe you shit."

"What do you want from me?" Xavier got to his feet, slapping his chest. He didn't care about the pain in his side. He'd had much worse injuries. "I've done everything you've ever asked."

The love of his life was in a coma, and he'd been the one to help put her there.

"Tell me what you need me to do."

Silence fell in the corridor. They weren't in a hospital but in a special ward that Boss owned.

"You need to leave this building right now."

"I'm not leaving her."

"You don't have a choice. You've done enough damage. Learn to keep your mouth shut."

"You're a fucking monster. You think I'm going to leave her with you?"

Boss slammed his fist against Xavier's nose, and he covered his face as blood started to spurt out of it. It was broken, no doubt about it.

"You think I'm the monster here?"

"You should have left her alone," said Xavier.

"You thought you were the one in charge. You could make all the decisions because what did I know? Huh? I don't know how to keep people safe?"

"You can't keep me from her, Boss. That's not your place."

"You fucked up this entire mission, Xavier. I can do whatever the hell I want, and as far as I'm concerned, *you* risked her life."

"You're just going to kill her. I won't let that happen."

"I'm not going to kill her, asshole. I'm going to protect her from herself. Keep her safe and that is far the fuck away from you. Get him out of my sight now. I don't want to see him here or anywhere else."

In the next second, he was being pulled down the long corridor. "Fuck this. No. Let me go. I swear, Boss, you do this and you make an enemy out of me."

"I'll add you to my long list."

Boss saluted him and walked back into the room with Alesha.

"No! Let me go."

It was no use. They had him in the elevator, a knife at his throat and he was traveling down toward the parking lot.

No.

He couldn't leave her.

Alesha.

He never intended for her to help with the hit.

This was all a big fuck-up. Boss already knew Xavier loved Alesha. Did he want him to come right out and say it?

The memory of the blood pooling around her, of her being unresponsive on the floor filled his head.

"You need to keep your cool right now," Killian said.

"I need to go to her."

"What you need to do is cool off, and you're not going to do that shit up there, you understand?" Bain said.

"If you don't let me go I'll make your wives widows, do you understand me?" He'd done his research on all of the Killer of Kings. If he was going to give his life to Boss, he intended to know who he was getting into bed with.

"You do that and you'll be dead within five minutes of leaving this building," Killian said. "I'd be careful who you threaten and take my advice."

The elevator doors opened up, and he was tossed out. There was no one to be seen.

"So that's it? You just let Boss win? He can't blame me for what happened." Xavier couldn't walk away.

"You think Boss wants this? You shouldn't have told her your plans. You should have done your job. The moment you signed on with Killer of Kings you agreed to this. Why do you think we follow him?" Killian shook his head. "He's a monster. We get that. He's a fucking bully and a bastard, but you know what, he has our best interests at heart. *You* put her life in danger today, not Boss." With that, Killian slammed his hand against the elevator button. "Get your shit together."

"What about the information on my sister?"

"Boss told me to tell you to get fucked," Bain

said.

The elevator doors closed and Xavier stared at them, and couldn't believe he'd been kicked out of the Killer of Kings tower. This shit shouldn't have happened. He wasn't the kind of bastard to be pushed aside.

Alesha could have died tonight because of him.

Running a hand down his face, he crouched down on the floor, feeling the pain strike him quick and fierce.

What the hell would he have done if she'd been killed?

Pulling his cell phone out of his pocket, he dialed Maurice's number.

It rang several times before it went to an answering machine. That had never happened. He didn't stop as he walked out of the building's parking lot onto the street. He dialed again and again until Maurice finally answered.

"I shouldn't be talking to you," Maurice said.

"Is that any way to talk to me?" Xavier asked.

"You're on the biggest shit list known to man. I'm thinking I should hang up."

"Wait. I need to know what Boss does in situations like this." He rubbed the back of his head, checking everyone he passed.

He was a known assassin that had just pissed off the boss of Killer of Kings. He wondered if Boss would order a hit on him.

"Look, I can't give you any of that information."

"I don't want trouble," Xavier said. "I need to know that she's going to be okay."

There was silence on the other end of the phone.

Patience wasn't exactly his strong suit right now, and it pissed him off that Maurice was being such a pain in the ass.

Mistakes like this never happened to him.

"Maurice, for fuck's sake, you know I'm good."

"Xavier, this has never happened before."

This made him pause. "Excuse me?"

"Look, everyone deals with their women differently. Boss has never had to invade a play like this, nor has he had to take care of a woman. She's a civilian and was at risk of being killed. She's been exposed to the traffickers you needed to bring down. Boss is taking care of her because he doesn't trust anyone else. This was supposed to be a clean mission. You should have kept her out of the loop. I don't know what Boss is going to do because it has never happened before. I'm sorry, Xavier, you really fucked this up, and everyone is pissed off."

With that, Maurice ended the call.

He stopped near a bench and lowered himself down on it with a groan.

Rubbing at his eyes, he couldn't think. Hitting his head repeatedly, he let out a scream, aware of the fact he was drawing attention. He didn't care. He needed to get the image of her out of his mind to know what to do next.

No matter what Boss said, he wasn't going to give up nor would he ever give in.

****

Alesha's mouth was dry, and something was stuck down her throat. She grabbed hold of the tube as a large man came into focus. She heard him trying to get her to stop, but she couldn't.

Xavier!

Where the hell was he?

She didn't have a clue where she was or what to do.

Her heart raced, and she heard machines beeping, letting her know that she had to be in some kind of hospital.

"Shit, she's a tough one, isn't she?"

"Boss, stop, you're going to freak her out."

"Alesha, listen to me. You have to be careful. You've been out of it for a few days. Take it easy. You're in safe hands. We're friends of Xavier's."

Hearing his name calmed her down enough for a nurse to come into the room. In the next few minutes, she finally had the tube out of her mouth and water placed in front of her. She sucked on the straw, drinking down the liquid as if it was a lifeline.

The man she vaguely recognized stayed in the room as the nurse asked her some really irritating questions.

She was asked her name, her age, what her favorite pet was. Stuff she didn't want to talk about.

"Where's Xavier?" she asked, turning to the man who stayed by her bed even as the nurse left the room.

"How are you feeling?" he asked.

"You heard how I'm feeling from the nurse and her twenty questions."

"You're rather prickly. I imagined El Diablo going for someone more timid, with a little less fire."

She stared at him. "Who are you?"

"Ah, I see you don't recognize me. I'm Boss."

She tried to think but could only think of Xavier talking about him. "You're Xavier's boss?"

"Something like that."

She rubbed at her head.

She already had a headache, and she'd been in this man's company less than five minutes.

So much had happened, and all the details were incredibly fuzzy.

"Where's Xavier?" she asked again.

The only person she wanted to see was the man who'd been by her side for some time now. The man she'd quickly grown to love.

"He's gone."

She stared at the man.

He had to be one of the largest men she'd ever seen. He looked so damn scary it sent a shiver up her spine.

"What do you mean he's gone?" she asked, trying to keep the tears in. Had he abandoned her? Was she damaged goods?

She didn't appear to be in a normal hospital even with all the machines. The man beside her was a stranger, Xavier nowhere in sight, everything was just too much.

"You need to calm down otherwise you're going to have a heart attack." Boss grabbed her wrist, feeling her pulse.

That didn't help to calm her down and only served to make her even more afraid.

"Please, I want to find Xavier."

"That won't be happening. For your safety and that of my investment."

"Investment?"

"Xavier is known as El Diablo. I have spent a long time trying to acquire him because he doesn't get attached. He has one focus in life, finding his sister. I can work with that. Use it to my advantage. I've got enough information to keep him working for me."

"You can't hold information of his sister over his head. That's not fair."

Boss tutted. "Why do women have to be so damn hormonal? I'll do whatever the hell I please. He was fierce, followed orders, and executed with an efficiency that impressed me. Then of course, you came along, didn't you? Messed with his fucking head and jeopardized our mission. You jumped in over your head and nearly got yourself killed."

She stared at the monster beside her.

How could Xavier work for him?

"I want to go to him."

"I'm a lot of things, Alesha, but I'm not a man who trusts easily. I'd like to keep my eye on you while you recover." Boss checked his watch. "How is the pain?"

She wouldn't talk to him.

Staring straight ahead of her, she tried to think of how to get out of here.

"You want to be stubborn? That's fine. I've dealt with many women in a worse state than you. I'm going to grab a cup of coffee. Don't even think to run. You won't get very far, and I don't like my patience tested."

Boss got up, and in the next second, she was alone.

She exhaled, her body slumping.

The only sound in the room was that of the beeping machine.

She swiped at her tears, finding them useless.

The only person she wanted was Xavier.

Sitting up in the bed, she started to pull out the wires that were hooked up to her. She cried out as she tore the needle that was stuck in her hand.

She didn't look forward to pain, but she'd rather deal with it than allow herself to cave to that bastard.

Pushing aside the blanket that covered her, she cursed. She wore a hospital gown and a quick glance at the back showed it was open. She wasn't wearing any underwear either.

Escape was her only solution. Putting her feet over the edge of the bed, she lifted herself off, and cried out at the pain. Her thigh was bandaged up, and as she lifted the gown, she saw there was also a bandage across her abdomen. The pain was intense.

"This is a really bad idea," she said.

She'd been shot in the thigh. Alesha recalled the panic in Xavier's voice as he screamed that she'd been hit. She'd also taken a bullet in her stomach. It had been much different than the luncheon. She should have minded her own damn business and let Xavier do his thing.

"Great, Alesha. You know how to mess things up." She'd gone to that dock to try to help Xavier, but ended up making everything worse.

She wasn't going to sit back and allow her injuries to keep her trapped. Using the bed for support, she took a step, trying to contain her whimpers. When she got to the edge of the bed, there wasn't anything for her to hold onto.

Alesha took another step, but her leg couldn't handle the pain and she dropped to the floor.

She felt dizzy and kept her head against the floor, hoping the cold tile would help her to focus.

She took several deep breaths.

In and out.

"Come on, Alesha, you can do this."

Eyes closed, she started to move her body toward the door, crawling, determined to win this. Dragging herself along the floor, the pain grew more intense, but she kept on going. The instant she was there, she knelt up and unlocked it. The door swung open, and she collapsed out.

"Have to keep going."

She dragged herself across the floor, hyperaware of the pain. When she looked down at her thigh, she saw the bandage covered in blood.

The stitches she had in her abdomen were also bleeding. Putting a hand to her stomach, she tried to think of what to do. There was no going back, only forward.

Pushing herself across the floor a little more, she had to rest.

"Xavier." She whimpered his name, hoping she'd be able to bring him with her begging of his name.

It didn't work.

"Shit! What the fuck are you doing?" Boss was back, and she looked up. He'd put his coffee on a tray and bent down.

"Xavier!" She cried out the name of the man she loved. Maybe he was nearby and would hear her.

Boss was the last man she wanted, but he picked her up in his arms as if she weighed nothing.

"Women will be the fucking death of me. What the heck is with you? Xavier put my whole mission in danger by talking to you. Hate me all you want, sweetheart, but I'm not sure what to do with either of you at this point."

"He didn't want me involved. It's my fault, not his."

He placed her so gently down on the bed it startled her. She didn't expect him to be so concerned for her.

"Get the nurse back here. She attempted to escape," Boss said, growling into his cell phone.

He shook his head before stepping away from the bed.

The nurse didn't take long. Apparently, Alesha had burst some of her stitches. She hated that Boss saw her in such a vulnerable position.

"You're going to have to rest!" The nurse glared at her. "I'm so over your patients, Boss. They're driving me crazy."

"You're paid well to do as you're told. Fuck off,"

Boss said.

"Does it hurt you to be nice to people?" Alesha asked.

"No. You're nice to people and they fuck you over. Simple as."

"So, you're not nice to anyone?"

"I pay well for the jobs I want. What more do people need?" Boss asked. He pushed a cart with a tray forward and wheeled it over to her so that she could eat. "Eat."

"Why can't you let Xavier come here? I don't understand."

"I'm pissed at him, and right now I want to kill him. If he comes here, I'll end up shooting him in the head."

She picked up the spoon and looked at Boss. He took a sip of his coffee, and she couldn't believe she was listening to him threaten the man she loved.

"Why didn't you run?" Boss asked.

"I just tried."

"No, when you learned the truth. You do know that there are many men and women out there that would pay a fortune for Xavier's location? He was passed out. You could be on a private island by now, basking in your riches."

She shrugged. "It didn't even enter my head. Besides, Xavier paid me to take care of his home. By extension, his home was part of him, so I took care of him as well. I'm not a snitch. I'm loyal."

"Yeah, at your own risk."

"You know where his sister is?" she asked.

Boss stared at her. "Yes."

"A good man would tell him where to find her."

"Newsflash, princess, I'm not a good man."

She rolled her eyes. "You're sitting with me, a

woman you don't know, to ensure I'm being taken care of. I think there's more to you than the asshole you try to show the world."

"So now you think you *understand* your boss's boss."

She couldn't help but smile. The nurse had put all the needles and monitor checks on her body that she'd taken off.

"This is so weird," Alesha said.

Silence fell between them. She ate some soup, finding it a little watery.

"Xavier is not ready to know the information I have. When he is, I will make sure he knows what I know."

She turned to Boss.

He stared at her hard.

She nodded.

He may not believe it, but Boss had a heart; he simply hid it well.

Chapter Eleven

Six weeks later

A knock on his door echoed in the early morning hours. Xavier pushed himself up in bed and checked the clock. It was two in the afternoon.

His head pounded. The late nights were getting to him.

He slipped on some shorts, grabbed a handgun from the top of his dresser, and went to answer the front door.

It was Viper, the last motherfucker he ever wanted to see. Maybe the second last.

"What do you want?"

"Boss wants to see you," he said.

"And I'm supposed to care? I'm not a dog he can call when he wants something. Remember, he's the one who cut me off, so I'm a free agent."

"Works for me. I'll tell him you refused." Viper turned to leave.

"Wait." Xavier swallowed his pride and took a cleansing breath. "Why does he want to see me?"

"Didn't ask."

"Is he letting me see Alesha?" It had been over a month since the day she'd been shot. He'd managed to get some information shortly after the incident, threatening one of the staff when they left for the night. Alesha's injuries were superficial—flesh wound to her thigh and grazed by a bullet on her stomach. Knowing her life wasn't in danger was the only thing keeping him grounded all this time.

"Like I said…"

"Fine. Give me a minute to get some clothes on."

Viper came inside and closed the door behind him, wandering around the expansive foyer. "Nice place."

"Yeah." Nothing material mattered without Alesha. He was completely in love with her. Xavier pulled on some pants and grabbed a shirt from his closet. After getting himself together, he returned to the front. "Where you taking me?"

"You'll be dealing with Boss. That's all you need to know."

Xavier adjusted his gun holster and slipped on his jacket. The other man watched him intently. "Why do you hate me so much?"

Viper's jaw twitched. "You're a loose cannon. You fucked up our last mission together. I know your history. If I can't trust you, you're not a friend, are you?"

"I was only trying to do the right thing. I'm not the man I used to be, or at least I was trying to change, to make a new life. You won't have it. None of you will give me a chance."

Viper shook his head. "Killer of Kings *is* our life. Not for you, though. You're only here because you want information from Boss. That isn't comforting to the men you're supposed to be working with. You don't get a second chance when it comes to life and death. It's a one-way trip if you don't have our backs."

"It was more than just getting information long before my training was through. For the first fucking time in my life I felt like I belonged, that I'd found my place. I guess I was wrong."

"Let's go."

He followed Viper out to his car and got in the passenger side. They hit the highway, and within minutes Viper's cell went off. After answering he handed it to Xavier.

"Still hotheaded?" asked Boss.

"No."

"Good. Time heals all wounds, eh?"

"What do you want? It's been six weeks without a word."

Xavier had been doing contracts as a free agent, trying to keep himself busy so he didn't obsess over Alesha. It was only a matter of time before he had her back, and he knew it. He'd never give up until he had her back. Boss couldn't hide her forever.

"You're not the average man, are you? I felt you needed some extra time to cool off and think about your actions. Maybe what you want out of life."

"I want Alesha. Nothing's changed."

"I thought you'd say that, which is why I have an offer for you."

He didn't like the sound of this. Offers from Boss hadn't gone over so well for him. He still didn't have his sister and he'd been with Killer of Kings nearly a year. "What is it?"

"I'm feeling generous today, so you have a choice. I release Alesha to you, but you continue to work for Killer of Kings."

"I thought you were done with me. You threw me the fuck out."

"You needed to cool off. Do you need more time for that?"

Xavier took a breath, calming his emotions. "No."

"Good. So, I can release Alesha to you and you continue to work for—"

"Fine, I'll do it," said Xavier. "I'll work for you. Follow all your orders."

"I wasn't finished," said Boss. "You take that offer *or* you get the location of your sister."

"What do you mean? You're making me choose?" He was shouting, but he didn't care at this point. "I was supposed to get information on Graciella after agreeing to work for you the first time."

"I gave you some information."

"An alias? A port of entry? What good did that do me?"

"*I* could have found her with that information. Make your choice, El Diablo. I don't have all day."

Since he was ten years old, he'd vowed to find the sister he was separated from. His entire life, she'd been in the back of his head. As an adult, he'd devoted countless resources into finding her. His sister had become an obsession.

Now he was being forced to make an impossible decision.

Boss was an evil bastard.

"Do you get a kick out of this shit? Does it give you a hard-on to tear me apart?"

"As far as I'm concerned, you should be kissing my ass for offering you anything. This is your get out of jail free card, so I'd shut the fuck up and take it before it's gone."

Xavier didn't have to think about it. "I'll take Alesha. Just make it happen."

There was silence on the line.

"Interesting."

"Where is she?"

"You'll continue working for Killer of Kings?"

"We've already been over the details," said Xavier. "You've kept her from me for nearly two months, and I don't want to wait another day."

"Put Viper on the line."

He tossed the phone back to the driver and then ran both hands through his hair. He hadn't tied it back today, too rushed to find out what Boss wanted from him. His mind wandered. Did Boss expect him to choose his sister? Was he disappointed he'd be working for him again? He wasn't sure what game Boss was playing, but he wanted no part of it. That man was screwing with his life, everything important to him, and it didn't make sense.

"We'll be there in ten," Viper told Xavier after putting the phone away.

Xavier watched the scenery flash by his passenger window, half in a daze.

"I thought you wanted to find your sister. That's how Boss got to work for him in the beginning, isn't it?"

He nodded.

"So why not take the information? You only hooked up with your housekeeper for a couple weeks. Doesn't make sense to me."

"I didn't *hook up* with her," he said. "How long did it take for you to know your woman was the one?"

Viper smirked, keeping his eyes on the road. "I was hired to kill her. Didn't turn out as planned."

"So how long?"

"Couple weeks, I guess. Maybe less."

"Exactly my point," said Xavier. "I've been searching for my sister my entire life. She's family, the only piece of my past I want to hold on to. But I'll sacrifice everything for Alesha. I just did. You should know how it is."

Viper tapped the steering wheel with a finger. "I never pegged you as a man to give a shit. Didn't think you had a loyal bone in your body."

"Well, there you go. I was labeled *the devil* most of my life because I had no other choice. It was survival of the fittest."

"Yeah, my childhood was pretty much what nightmares are made of. Seems to be a common thread with Boss's men."

Xavier shrugged. "If a guy grew up in the suburbs with a silver spoon in his mouth, he'd be white collar, not killing for a living."

"Good point."

The tension between them eased. It seemed choosing Alesha over garnering information had earned him points with Killer of Kings.

They pulled into the front drive of a posh hotel a while later. Boss likely owned it. He controlled half the damn city. Before Xavier could get out of the car, the revolving door revealed Alesha. She stood there in a navy-blue dress, her hair fluttering loosely in the slight breeze.

He exited the car, but stopped abruptly on the sidewalk, worried if she even wanted to see him. Maybe she hated him for involving her in his madness. Maybe Boss had brainwashed her.

They were both frozen in time, staring at each other. She was fucking gorgeous, the sun highlighting her baby blue eyes.

Her mouth opened, but no words came out, and then she ran. She rushed toward him. As soon as she thrust herself into his arms, he picked her arm, twirling her briefly. He held her tight, relief that she hadn't rejected him filling him with calm. He had her back.

"Xavier." She kissed him all over the face, dozens of individual kisses.

"Baby, I'm never letting you go."

"I've missed you," she said, leaning back to look at him.

He lowered her to her feet. "How you healing?"

"I'm fine. What I needed was you."

"Boss kept me away. I wanted to be here, I swear to you."

She ran her hands over his chest. "I know. Can

we get away from here?"

He glanced over at Viper, and the hitman nodded. "Yeah, let's get out of here."

This was perfect, a new start at forever. But Xavier couldn't shake the sinking feeling he was missing something crucial. Boss was complicated and twisted. Xavier didn't like how easy this was, even if Boss continued to withhold information about his sister. All he knew was he couldn't make any mistakes. Any more screw ups and next time Boss could keep Alesha from him forever.

They sat in the backseat of Viper's car together. He ran his hand through her hair, still in shock he had her back. "Did they hurt you?"

She shook her head.

He pulled up the hem of her dress to see her thigh. The stitches were healing nicely. He trailed his fingers lightly over the scar. "I'm so sorry, Alesha."

"It was my choice. You didn't want to involve me, so don't blame yourself," she said. "Besides, the doctors said I'd be as good as new in no time. A bit of a limp, but I think it's more habit at this point."

"I messed up. You're mine to protect."

His guilt wouldn't let him go. He expected she'd stay at home, not follow him into danger.

Xavier noticed they weren't going in the direction of his house. He sat straighter, looking to both sides.

"What's wrong?" she asked.

"Viper, you forget where I live already?"

"Just doing my job. Nothing personal."

His hackles bristled. "Where we going?" He rested his hand on the handle of his Glock inside his jacket.

"Boss has an assignment for you. Both of you, actually."

"No way. She just got out of the damn hospital. Has Boss lost his damn mind?"

"It was a hotel. One of the best. Not a hospital." Viper tossed an envelope into the backseat. Xavier opened it and started shuffling through the contents.

"I'm not prepared for this," he said.

Viper appeared unfazed. "If you work for Killer of Kings, you always have to be prepared. Since you've been on vacay, the rest of us have cleaned up most of the human smuggling operation. There are only three players left. Boss wants you to finish this personally."

He did want to see them all fry. Eliminating the complete cell meant Alesha would be safer and off the radar. "It's too dangerous for Alesha. I'll handle this. Take her home."

"Sorry, buddy. Boss was very explicit. Besides, it's high-end private club. You'll be fine," said Viper. "Your memberships are in the envelope, along with the hits."

"There are only two pictures. Who's the third?"

"Boss will give Alesha the third player in thirty minutes. There's a cell phone in the woman's washroom that she'll need to grab. Boss's insurance policy that you follow orders."

He cursed under his breath, but kept his comments to himself. Boss wanted loyalty. He wanted to ensure Xavier would bend over backwards, regardless of Alesha. He'd play the role, but he wouldn't put the mission above Alesha for anyone.

She squeezed his thigh, grounding him. He turned to look at her. "It'll be okay, Xavier. I'm not afraid."

He smiled. "Of course, you aren't." Xavier leaned over and brushed his lips over hers. Within seconds the kiss deepened, and he moved closer, needing more.

Viper cleared his throat.

"We're here. Good luck. There's a bag in the trunk for you."

"Will you be waiting?"

Viper shifted in his seat after parking. "Chains is on standby. Give him a text when you're through. I have to help Pepper set up for our kid's birthday party tomorrow."

It sounded crazy, mixing the life of a hitman with family commitments, but it's exactly what Xavier hoped to achieve with Alesha. This was their own twisted version of reality at Killer of Kings.

He helped Alesha out of the car, grabbed the duffel bag from the trunk, and together they walked to the private club. He hoped this was the last test Boss subjected him to.

****

Absence did make her heart grow fonder. As soon as Alesha saw Xavier, everything in her world felt right. She'd felt like Rapunzel, locked in a tower, waiting for her knight to save her. Boss wouldn't even let her call him. He was an enigma.

Alesha sensed a darkness within Boss. Something dangerous and inhuman. He was also intelligent, always one step ahead of everyone. A lethal combination. He'd told her he was keeping her away for Xavier's benefit, for the whole of Killer of Kings. It didn't make sense. He kept telling her a big day was coming. She thought he was talking about her reuniting with Xavier, but it was something bigger, and it scared her.

At first, she thought Boss hated Xavier, but she soon learned that he respected him, and saw him as a prize, some kind of trophy for his organization. He seemed to be collecting the worst of the worst to do his bidding. Only a monster could control such a group. He'd have to be worse.

"I don't want you involved, Alesha. Stay by the door while I scope out the place," said Xavier, holding her had as they neared the front doors.

"You heard what Viper said. I have to get the phone from the woman's bathroom. He'll expect to hear from me. I won't screw this up for us."

He scowled, but opened the door for her to enter. She was expecting a golf and country club, but this place was way above her pay grade. It seemed to be a social club for all the old money of the city. She felt completely out of her element.

Xavier walked in like he owned the place.

He stood tall, scanning the room, looking for his targets. She felt safe next to him. She hoped she didn't get shot today. Her recovery hadn't been fun, but she'd always been good with pain.

An employee in a full suit approached them. Xavier didn't even speak, just handed him the memberships.

"It's wonderful to have you with us, Mr. and Mrs. Moreno. Please enjoy your stay."

Once the man walked off, a woman took his place, holding a tray of champagne flutes. Xavier shook his head and she left.

"How does it feel to be called Mrs. Moreno?" he asked.

He had no idea. She'd give anything to belong to him. "It feels nice."

They linked arms, and they walked around the club. There were a few couples, but mostly groups of men with lots of cash on tables, scantily clad women hanging off them. She quickly realized this wasn't a place for the white-collar elite but the criminal underworld.

"I see one of them," he whispered, not looking at

her. She followed his gaze and recognized the man from that day at the docks. He'd been the one smoking a cigar on the sofa.

"He'll recognize me," she said. Her heartrate was already on the up climb and they'd only just shown up.

"Why don't you visit the ladies' room, darling," he said aloud, pointing to the door down a narrow hallway.

She nodded, glad to get away to calm her nerves. The cell phone was supposed to be hiding, duct-taped under the counter. When she entered the bathroom, there were other women inside, so she pretended to use the toilet. Once the coast was clear, she slipped out of the stall and felt around under the sinks. It hurt to squat down, so she kept pawing around for the phone when it started ringing.

Her heart jumped, and she quickly retrieved it and put it to her ear. "Hello?" she whispered.

"You can speak normally, Alesha. People use the phone in the bathroom all the time."

"Sorry."

"I'm going to tell you two words. You'll understand when the time comes. Don't say anything until then," said Boss.

"Until when? What's going on here?"

"I like things to happen organically. With a little help, of course. People don't learn unless they experience things firsthand. When my men think I'm out to destroy them, I'm just teaching a lesson or opening their eyes to something they couldn't see on their own."

"You're not making any sense."

"Widow Maker. Those are your words. Now go off and mingle. I hear you're a good actress." The line went dead.

Fuck.

When she exited the bathroom, the door of the men's room across the hall slammed shut, making her jump. There was more banging, but she continued down the hall. She went in search of Xavier, not finding him where she left him. Within seconds, his arms snaked around her waist from behind. He kissed her neck, reminding her how capable of a lover he was. It had been two long months, and she just wanted to be alone with him. No more drama.

"Where were you?"

"Just using the restroom."

She turned around in his arms. "The man we saw?"

"Taken care of. One down, two to go. Did you get the call you were waiting for?"

She nodded. Damn, he worked fast. His skills turned her on, her body already thrumming. He backed her up in a quiet corner, then lifted up the edge of her dress.

"What are you doing?"

He shut her up with a kiss—deep and passionate. She closed her eyes and absorbed his masculine scent. One hand squeezed her ass, while the other snaked under her dress and into the front of her panties. Before she could protest again, he'd impaled two fingers deep into her cunt. She gasped aloud, grabbing his shoulders to keep from collapsing.

A couple people walked down the hall behind them, but no one seemed to care what they were doing. Being so naughty out in the open was oddly titillating. Her clit throbbed, heat rushing out from her womb to her extremities.

Xavier finger-fucked her as he trailed kisses down her neck.

"Did you miss me, baby?"

"Oh God." She panted, craving his cock. "Are you acting, Xavier?"

"Never with you." He kissed her forehead and pulled away. "Tonight, I'll show you something new." He winked, and her heart did a flip. She'd wanted him to fuck her right there against the wall. That's how much he pulled her from reality with each kiss.

They strolled around, pretending to mingle, her body still wired. A live band played in the adjoining room, a mix of violin, harp, and piano. A few couples danced nearby.

Xavier held her by his side as they enjoyed the music. It almost felt like a date—minus the dead guy in the bathroom and another kingpin on his radar.

Then Alesha saw her. Her heart stopped for a moment. She squeezed Xavier's hand. It must be her, the third hit, the one Boss told her about on the phone.

"What's wrong?" asked Xavier.

Her mouth felt like cotton, and it took her a while to get the words out. "It's her," she said. "Widow Maker."

It was the beautiful woman from the yacht. The one who'd saved her from Dixon. It didn't make any sense.

Xavier's entire body tensed, and he looked to the woman on the dance floor in the red skirt. Then Alesha noticed the man she danced with was their second hit. They must be a couple.

Xavier took a step back, and when she checked his expression, there was something distressed in his gaze. He reminded her of a child, lost and confused. She touched his chest, desperate to heal him.

"You don't have to do this right now," she tried to comfort. "If it's too much for you—"

"You don't understand," he said. "The Widow

Maker is my sister."

Chapter Twelve

The Widow Maker led the man off the dance floor. There's no way Xavier was letting her out of his sight. Not now. Not after all this time. Keeping hold of Alesha's hand, he moved through the throngs of people keeping her in his line of sight.

"I don't think we should be following her."

"I'm not letting her get away." He kept a hand on his gun, Alesha at his back, and ready to take on anything.

He smiled as he passed people, always playing his part. In the time he'd been away, he'd learned there were rules to follow with Killer of Kings. Lives were always at risk, and he had to be ready to take on the entire fucking world if he could.

"This is not a good idea, Xavier."

"I don't give a fuck what it is. Boss did this on purpose. He gave me a choice. You or her. I'm not going to let him hurt her." Knowing Boss, he had already signed her death certificate.

"Boss is not all bad, you know. He's not going to hurt you just for the sake of hurting you."

"You're an expert now?" Xavier asked.

"Are you being a pain in the ass on purpose right now? Calm down, Xavier."

He wasn't going to calm down. That was his sister. She'd been a ghost for thirty years. He couldn't just walk away.

They entered the far corridor. No one was around.

Suddenly, he heard a thud.

All of his senses went on high alert. He made Alesha hold his jacket as he made his way to the door, kicking it open, he held his gun and stared into the eyes of his sister.

For a split second he was transported back to the day she was pulled out of his arms. Her screams for help filling the air. The utter failure he experienced at knowing he didn't fight hard enough. He'd only been a boy.

Only, the eyes he stared back were no longer filled with fear. She held a garrote. The man, one of his hits, had it wrapped around his neck and was choking to death. She didn't even look as if she was fighting all that hard to take the life from him. Seconds passed, and Widow Maker smiled at him. Graciella Moreno.

"Hello, brother mine. Long time, no see."

The man in her arms collapsed. She let him go.

He dropped to the floor dead.

"Graciella."

She wrinkled her nose. "It has been a long time since I was called that name. I go by Widow Maker, if people live long enough to say it, Xavier."

"I've been looking for you all over."

"Not very hard. I've been around for a long time. Enough to see the mistakes you're making."

"What the hell happened to you?"

"A lot of things. Stuff I don't talk about. We can't talk here. This is a hot zone, and I want to live. I know Boss led you here and all, but this is my kill. He's an interfering bastard. If he thinks for a second, I'm going to do what he wants, he's got another think coming." Before he could react, Graciella moved past him.

There was no way he couldn't follow her.

"Don't even think of getting rid of me," Alesha said. "We've been apart too long. Besides, I'd really like to get to know your sister before she kills you."

"She's not going to kill me."

"I hate to break it to you, Xavier, but she looked pissed off."

Ignoring Alesha, he held her hand and followed Graciella out of the building. She'd killed the other hit smoothly without anyone even noticing. The body slumped in the corner looking as if he'd drunk too much.

His sister was an expert. No wonder Boss didn't have a problem following after her. She'd fit right in at Killer of Kings.

"I'll follow you to your home," Graciella said.

"We can meet at a coffee shop." He didn't want her to go. This was the first time he'd seen his sister in ages. She was a woman now, strong, nothing like he remembered.

"Not safe. I've got to change, and right now, I need to blend. I'll be at your home at five." Graciella turned on her heel, about to go.

"Don't," he said. "Don't go."

Graciella sighed. "I don't have time for all this neediness, Xavier. You see me. I've been alive a long time. Believe me, I know how to take care of myself. I don't need my brother attempting to do that. I'll meet you back at your place."

He watched her go.

Alesha was still by his side.

The mission completed.

His world put right and once again in fucking turmoil.

"Xavier?"

"Come on, let's get you home before Boss decides to change his fucking mind." He wouldn't put it past that son of a bitch to make him pay somehow.

She didn't argue with him as he helped her in the car.

Neither of them spoke during the visit back to his home. Once inside, he locked all the doors, and his cell phone rang.

The caller didn't have any details on his phone, but he answered it anyway. Alesha headed to the kitchen, and he followed behind her.

"Hello," he said.

"Why do you sound so fucking miserable? I give you what you want and you're still pissed?" Boss asked.

"You knew Graciella would be there."

"Of course. I couldn't exactly give you everything at once. I wanted to see how much you cared about your woman. The other men needed to see you had a loyal bone in your body. Ask Alesha if she's missing me."

"She's not."

"You didn't ask her. I'm a pretty decent guy once you get to know me."

"I have no intention of ever getting to know you. What the fuck do you want?" he asked.

Boss tsked. "I take it Widow Maker wasn't accommodating."

"You've known who she is all this time?"

"Of course. Nothing gets past me, and I already gave you all the info to find her. The simple truth, Xavier, is you were too scared to find her."

"Fuck you."

Alesha put her hands on his shoulders, offering him the comfort and support he needed. Right now, his mind was all over the place.

Boss laughed. "Let's face it, Xavier. She doesn't need you. She'll never need you. Out of the two of you, she's the deadlier assassin. I hope you enjoy what you've found out." With that, Boss hung up.

Tossing the phone away, Xavier watched as it hit the wall shattering to pieces.

"Are you okay?"

"That was my sister, Alesha. I haven't seen her in

so long. She was innocent, a terrified little girl, and I failed her."

"You didn't fail me," Graciella said, leaning around the corner of the door.

Xavier stood straight.

She had changed, her hair up in a long ponytail, sunglasses pushed up on her head. There was a smile to her lips. She wore a leather jacket, tight trousers, and a pristine white shirt.

She stepped into the room, taking a seat. "I could imagine you living in a place like this. It's nice. Just what my brother would order."

"You don't know me."

"But I do. I know all about Xavier and El Diablo. I've kept an eye on you over the years. You've had some really good hits."

"What happened to you?"

Graciella smiled, but it didn't reach her eyes. "What happens to most young girls who are taken? The worst possible thing. I was sold on the black market. Turns out a lot of men liked the prospect of fucking a child. So, you can use your imagination. The story goes on until I was tossed out on the streets in England. My body a bloody mess. My life ruined. My hopes gone. One man, he helped me. He wasn't interested in my body, but he liked my fighting spirit. He told me that if I worked for him, everyone that had ever done me harm would face the consequences." She held her hands up. "It was an offer I couldn't resist. Of course, he had his own reasons for wanting me around. There were men he wanted me to kill. He couldn't do it himself. He provided all the money I needed." The smile on her lips died. "Of course, I should have known it wouldn't end with him. He was one of the men who helped to sell boys and girls. I couldn't let him live."

"That's not the full story," Xavier said.

"Of course it's not. You don't get to have the full story. All you need to know is I lived a life of hell and came back from it. That's what I do. I've got more kills under my belt than you have. I'm not the sweet little sister anymore. She died one night after being used. I can't give you what you were looking for."

"But you knew I was looking for you?"

"Of course." Graciella reached out, taking his hand. "I know you were hoping to be the winner in this story. The hero. I don't need a hero. I'm a fighter. I take care of all my own battles, and I hope one day, you can be … happy for me."

He hated this. "I love you, Graciella. I'm so sorry that I failed you. None of that shit should ever have happened."

The smile was back. "You haven't failed me." She looked at Alesha. "Take care of my brother. Make sure he's loved and protected."

"Yes."

"Good."

"Wait, you can't go," Xavier said. This reunion was decades in the making. She'd been through more hell than he could have imagined, and he wanted to undo all the horrors.

"The world never sleeps for me. I've got to go, otherwise I'll end up as one of Boss's minions. That bastard will *not* stop when he wants something. I much prefer keeping one step ahead and taking the contracts from under his nose."

"You could become part of Killer of Kings."

Graciella grimaced. "I hate to say this, but they're a little too tame for me. Besides, I work on my own. Nothing in this world is easy, and I don't have time to get attached. We'll talk again soon."

He watched her get to her feet. Heard her heels clicking on the floor, and he didn't follow her. The Graciella he knew, she wasn't there at the moment. He hoped she wasn't gone forever. But El Diablo had managed to find peace, and so could she.

Alesha rested her head on his shoulder. "It'll be okay. I promise," she said.

"I've got you. I know I'll be fine."

She cupped his face and made him turn to look at her. "I've missed you so much."

"Boss said you enjoyed his company."

She rolled her eyes. "He thinks he's a comedian. Believe me, he's not even close to being funny. I just wanted to be with you. To stay here. To love you." She stroked his cheek. "Please tell me we can be together now. No more secrets?"

"Well, you've met my family. That's all I have to offer."

"I think your sister likes me."

"She's gone, Alesha. She really is gone." Her quick disappearance after just finding her hit him like a blow to the gut.

"She'll come back."

"How do you know that?"

Alesha held him tight against her chest, the soft cushions of her tits still so inviting.

"Because she cares enough to come and see you. If she really didn't, she wouldn't have been here."

He pulled Alesha into his arms, pressing his face against her neck, breathing her in. This was home. She was his woman, and he loved her more than anything.

"I'm never letting you go."

"Good, because I don't want to go anywhere."

****

Two months later

"Don't drop me. Please don't drop me," Alesha said, giggling as Xavier held her a little bit tighter against his body.

After they'd had the tackiest wedding possible in Vegas, with Boss, several of the guys at Killer of Kings, as well as his sister present, he'd decided to piggyback her to their hotel. They'd made it into the elevator, and he refused to let her go.

She couldn't stop laughing as he rested her against the wall of the elevator and his body. With her arms draped across his chest, she'd tightened her hold as the elevator doors slid open and she had no choice but to go with him as they walked toward their room.

Boss had given her away. The truth was, she *had* enjoyed his company during her extended stay with the man. Although she'd never had the displeasure of witnessing the dark side so many spoke about.

He was all hard ass and bad attitude, but she had found him to be wonderful. He had a sweet side, and he did try to hide it—and failed miserably.

"I'm not going to drop you."

"Then what is taking so long with the key?"

The door opened, but Xavier wasn't done with his mission yet. She groaned as he carried her through to the bedroom. He'd kicked the door shut on the way inside, and she kept holding onto him, feeling like a child and so full of life.

He turned and suddenly dropped her … a few inches from the mattress.

She let out a scream and burst out laughing. "That has to be the weirdest way a bride has been carried over the threshold."

"We're not home yet. I've got a whole new plan for that."

"You have?"

"Yep."

Alesha watched him as he began to loosen his tie. Even when he pissed her off, she still found him to be one of the sexiest men she'd ever seen.

"Do you like what you see?"

"It's okay." She smiled at him.

"Get up. Take your clothes off."

"That's it? Just get naked?" she asked.

"I want you completely naked because for the next two days, your ass is not seeing any clothes."

He put his hands on her knees, leaned in close and kissed her.

"Do you promise?"

"Babe, you're my wife now. Mrs. Moreno. The love of my fucking life. I'm not going to let you go, ever." He kissed her again before pulling her to her feet. "Now, I want you to strip naked. To show me your body because I'm going to kiss every inch of it and then I'm going to fuck you in so many different ways, you won't be able to see straight."

She stood up and presented her back to him so that he could take care of the zipper. He slid it down her body, and she wriggled out of the dress. It was simple, but stunning, more than she could have dreamed of for her wedding. Turning to stand in front of him in her white lingerie, she heard him moan.

"Do you like what you see?" she asked, repeating the same question he'd asked her just moments ago.

Xavier shoved his pants down, showing off his large cock. Already the tip was wet with his pre-cum. "What do you think?" He ran his hand up and down, going from the base up to the root, and back down again. "You know what I want?"

She nodded.

"On your knees, baby."

When she made to take off her panties and bra, Xavier stopped her. "I'll deal with them."

She sank to her knees, and Xavier stepped up close, his cock near her mouth. Staring up at him, she opened her lips, wrapping her fingers around the length, and she tasted him. The musky scent of his pre-cum glided across her tongue. Moaning his name around his girth, she took him to the back of her throat. He'd taught her exactly how best to do this. What he liked.

She cupped his balls with her free hand, playing with them, teasing them. His cock seemed to swell in her mouth, and as she sucked him down, he growled.

"Our first time tonight is not going to be with me coming down that pretty throat." He pulled her off his cock, picking her up. His fingers were still in her hair as he held her in place, ravishing her lips.

He broke the kiss as he spun her around. His hand moved between her thighs, cupping her pussy. He tugged on the thin fabric of her panties, tearing them from her.

His hand was once again on her sex without anything between them. She wriggled back and forth, craving his cock. She loved his hands all over her, the scent of his cologne, and roughness of his touch.

He slid a finger through her slit, moving down to plunge inside her. She cried out his name. Her *husband's* name.

Xavier wasn't done as he pressed her to the bed. The tip of his cock pressed at her entrance as he slid in deep. Gripping the sheet beneath her, she tried to hold onto her sanity, but Xavier was driving her crazy. His fingers teased her clit at the same time he rocked his cock within her. She felt so full, so fully taken by her man.

"Look at us, baby. See my cock going so deep inside you. That's a fucking beautiful sight. So fucking pretty."

Alesha turned her head, and there across from the bed was a massive mirror. She saw them both. The erotic scene excited her. Xavier's body was hard, and she couldn't stop staring.

Xavier pulled out enough so that she could see his cock. It was already wet with her arousal.

He pushed inside her, and she gasped. He was so deep, his erection throbbing.

"I'm not going to fucking last. Not after having those sweet lips around my dick. Fuck, baby, you are all mine. All fucking mine." He pounded inside her, stroking her pussy, bringing her to the edge. She panted, the pressure growing higher and higher, and then she leapt over the edge. His name tumbled off her lips, like it always did.

This man.

This crazy assassin was now hers.

In the eyes of the law.

In their eyes.

She was his, and he was hers.

Xavier followed her into bliss, his cock swelling as he fucked her harder, going deeper as wave upon wave of cum spilled inside her.

He leaned over her, his lips at her neck as he sucked on her pulse. "This is just the start."

She gasped as he pulled out of her. In the next second, even as his cum leaked from her pussy, he carried her through to the bathroom.

He turned on the shower, and he pulled her beneath the cold water with him. She let out a squeal, and he laughed.

"Xavier, what the hell?"

"I'm protecting my woman."

"Not from getting cold." She wiped the water from her eyes. When her vision was clear once again, she saw him smiling.

It wasn't just any kind of smile though. This one was genuine, filled with love. It was the kind of smile that she'd only ever seen him give to her.

"What is it?" she asked.

"I never thought there would come a day when I'd be so happy."

"You're happy?"

"Yes, Alesha." He cupped her face. "You have no idea."

He didn't need to tilt her head back as she was already staring at him.

"You make me so happy. Seeing you today, knowing that you gave up the idea of a sweet church wedding, it did something to me."

Three days ago, she'd stormed into the house, angry at everything. The church they'd arranged to have their wedding had rearranged their dates three times. The flowers she wanted were a ridiculous price, and the woman refused to make her a lemon cake for her wedding. The bridal shops she went to had been rude to her about her size. Then, of course, the actual guests were hard to pin down. As Xavier had warned, there was a risk of not all the guests being able to attend.

Organizing her wedding wasn't supposed to be stressful.

She had told him that she was done trying to give him the perfect wedding. Within three days, they were in Vegas, with a few of their guests … and it had been perfect. They had shared a cream cake with each other. It was a day that many would have hated, but for Alesha, it had been a dream come true.

So long as she was with Xavier, what did the details matter?

Who cared if they had the right flowers or the

correct church, or the right meal? To her, it didn't matter at all. So long as he loved her and she him, nothing else mattered.

"I'll never forget this day for as long as I live, Alesha. I want you to know that." He licked his lips. "Where I came from, what I've been through—I thought I was lost. I hated the world and myself. You showed me what real love is."

She grabbed his arms, turning him around and pressing him against the cool tiles. He let out a growl. She chuckled. "See, it's so cold."

"I'm trying to share my heart with you and you're not listening."

Alesha ran her hands down his muscled chest. "I am listening to you."

"These words, they don't come naturally to me."

"I know." She pressed a kiss to his lips. "You don't have to say them."

"I know, but I want to. I know life with me, it's hard. You deserve more." There were weeks where he'd disappear for days at a time. She'd lie in their bed, waiting to hear from him. Xavier had told her many times that it didn't matter how far away he went, there was always someone watching her. She was taken care of.

For her, that didn't bother her.

What she cared about was knowing *he* was safe. And he was never gone for long.

"I can't promise you life is going to be easy with me. I imagine there are going to be times that you hate me. I'll hate myself even more." He ran his thumb across her lips. "You are my world. My love. My everything. I was only half a man when I met you. You complete me."

It sounded like he'd practiced this.

"Are these … are these your vows?"

"Yes," he said. "I wanted to say them to you earlier, but they didn't seem to fit the mood."

She took his hand in hers and kissed his wrist. "There's nothing else you need to say. For richer or poorer, I love you. I'll stay by your side. I will be your loyal servant for the rest of our lives." She took his hand and placed it against her stomach.

He looked at his hand and then at her.

"Are you trying to tell me something right now?" he asked.

"I'm pregnant, Xavier. We're going to have a baby."

"Oh fuck, we're going to be parents?"

"Yes."

She laughed as he lifted her up. His lips on hers. She wrapped her arms around his neck, knowing that no matter what life threw at them, so long as they had each other, they were going to be okay.

"Fuck, do you need to lie down? Do I need to call the doctor?"

"No, Xavier, you just need to be the man I love."

The End

www.samcrescent.com

www.staceyespino.com

CPSIA information can be obtained
at www.ICGtesting.com
Printed in the USA
LVHW091047070719
623231LV00001BA/36/P